Horatio Alger, Jr. (1832–99), the son of a Unitarian minister, was born in Massachusetts. After studying at Harvard, Alger pursued a career in the ministry before moving to New York City, where he began writing his successful books for boys such as *Luck and Pluck, Tattered Tom, Phil the Fiddler,* and *Struggling Upward.* His eighth novel, *Ragged Dick,* was his first of many bestsellers.

Michael Meyer, PhD, is a professor of English at the University of Connecticut. Among his books, *Several More Lives to Live: Thoreau's Political Reputation in America* was awarded the Ralph Henry Gabriel Prize by the American Studies Association. In addition to *The Bedford Introduction to Literature,* his edited volumes include *Frederick Douglass: The Narrative and Selected Writings.*

Bryan Waterman is Associate Professor of English and American Literature at New York University and coeditor, with Cyrus R. K. Patell, of *The Cambridge Companion to the Literature of New York City.*

RAGGED DICK

or, Street Life in New York with the Boot Blacks

Horatio Alger, Jr.

WITH AN INTRODUCTION BY
MICHAEL MEYER
AND A NEW AFTERWORD BY
BRYAN WATERMAN

SIGNET CLASSICS

SIGNET CLASSICS
Published by the Penguin Group
Penguin Group (USA) LLC, 375 Hudson Street,
New York, New York 10014

USA | Canada | UK | Ireland | Australia | New Zealand | India | South Africa | China
penguin.com
A Penguin Random House Company

Published by Signet Classics, an imprint of New American Library,
a division of Penguin Group (USA) LLC

First Signet Classics Printing, September 1990
First Signet Classics Printing (Waterman Afterword), July 2014

Ⓒ REGISTERED TRADEMARK—MARCA REGISTRADA

ISBN 978-0-451-46959-5

Printed in the United States of America
10 9 8 7 6 5 4 3 2 1

Introduction

HORATIO ALGER, JR., wrote more than one hundred books for boys during the last third of the nineteenth century until his death in 1899. He was a prodigious, though limited, writer whose output and impact surpassed his talents as a novelist. Although Alger stood only five feet two inches tall—just about the size of the boys who were his audience—he achieved unexpected stature in American literary history owing to his enormous readership. The vagaries of nineteenth-century book publishing and their inflated sales records led early enthusiastic biographers of Alger to contend erroneously that he was better known in America than Shakespeare and that he outsold Dickens, Thackeray, Hemingway, and Faulkner combined. Estimates of his total sales have been as high as a half billion, but more realistic informed guesses come in below twenty million. The cheap editions reissued after Alger's death account for the majority of these sales until the 1920s, when his popularity waned. Even so, that's a lot of books that were bought, passed around among readers, and borrowed from libraries.

Almost no one writes about these novels without quickly apologizing for the quality of Alger's prose, but it is also true that the influence of his juvenile books is simultaneously richly acknowledged, because, even though they are mostly no longer read, their sheer existence and significance cannot be overlooked by literary historians and cultural critics. If all of his individual books were stacked in one pile alongside their author, they would tower more than three feet above his head, and in that curious image, one could visualize the paradox of his teetering reputation: not many readers are actually familiar with Alger's life or writing yet almost everyone has read or heard allusions to his novels.

For the one hundred fiftieth anniversary of Alger's birth in Chelsea, Massachusetts, the *New York Times* reported that the United States Postal Service had issued a twenty-cent commemorative stamp featuring four boys dressed as New York City street vagrants from his Ragged Dick series. The *Times* article's lead paragraph succinctly summarizes how Alger left his mark on literary history: "It is a measure of Horatio Alger's imprint on America that his name has become part of the language—when we describe a man's life as a 'Horatio Alger story' no one doubts that the man rose from poverty through virtue and hard work to achieve success and riches and thus realize the American Dream" (May 2, 1982). Although Alger's heroes are often mistakenly assumed to amass great "riches" on the order of a John Rockefeller, Andrew Carnegie, Cornelius Vanderbilt, or Jay Gould, they achieved a much more modest kind of success consisting of middle-class respectability. The *Times* description nonetheless captures the popular reputation of the stories by pointing to Alger's abiding emphasis on his heroes' perseverance and determination to get ahead. Alger's reputation is so subsumed by this essential plot that his name is often mistakenly thought to refer to one of the fictional characters in his stories of self-made American boys.

Distinguishing between the real Horatio Alger and the fictional version is a complicated task in Alger studies, because his first biographer, Herbert R. Mayes, based his life of Alger on made-up incidents, gleeful lies, and fake diaries as well as letters that Mayes wrote himself. In 1928 Mayes published *Alger: A Biography Without a Hero* as a parody of debunking biographies that were popular in the 1920s. He never intended his phony accounts of Alger as an obsessively ambitious neurotic who has desperate escapades and affairs with mistresses to be taken seriously. As he publicly explained some forty years later when he acknowledged the hoax, he wrote a parody because he couldn't find enough information to write a genuine biography. To his own surprise, his work was accepted as the truth about Alger until the 1970s, because no reviewers seriously challenged his fabricated biography and, even worse, because it became the basis of the 1928 entry on Alger in the *Dictionary of American Biography.* This standard reference work had a powerful distorting influence on subsequent treatments of his life. Mayes created a fictitious personality for Alger that was eagerly accepted by readers who were delighted to believe that the moralistic writer of boys' books was, ironically, a dissolute fraud and miserable failure.

Mayes' biography without a hero (or facts) represents a bizarre chapter in American literary history because many subsequent critics and biographers drew upon it for their work. John Tebbel's 1963 biography, for example, *From Rags to Riches: Horatio Alger and the American Dream,* relies heavily on Mayes and actually claims to make additional use of the nonexistent diary from which Mayes supposedly quoted. Further complicating the problem, Ralph D. Gardner's *Horatio Alger, or The American Boy Era* (1964) and Edwin P. Hoyt's *Horatio's Boys* (1974) repeat Mayes' fictions, and, astonishingly, add their own made-up incidents and misinformation. All of this is thoroughly detailed in *The*

Lost Life of Horatio Alger, Jr. by Gary Scharnhorst (with Jack Bales). Published in 1985 and carefully researched, this is the latest and most reliable biography to date, and it should be the starting point for any serious study of Alger, given that scholarly and popular treatments of him sometimes continue to draw upon earlier inaccurate sources. Scharnhorst cuts through the layers of misinformation and provides the known facts of Alger's life.

As even a thumbnail sketch demonstrates, Alger's life is both more complicated and surprising than Mayes ever imagined. Alger grew up in a privileged social environment much different from that of the newsboys and bootblacks who populated the grimy city streets in his fiction. His father was a Unitarian minister who barely made a meager but genteel living but who nevertheless managed to send his son to Harvard College, from which Horatio graduated in 1852 as a member of Phi Beta Kappa. For the next five years this promising beginning was tempered by a series of false starts as Alger worked at being a serious writer, divinity school student, newspaper editor, schoolteacher, and private tutor. In 1857 he reenrolled in the Harvard Divinity School and graduated in 1860, when he continued to support himself by writing sentimental moralistic fiction, poetry, and essays for a variety of magazines. These only modest successes led him in 1864 to accept an appointment as a minister at the First Unitarian Church in Brewster, Massachusetts, and to focus on writing literature for juveniles rather than for adults because it paid better. In effect, he abandoned his attempts to be a serious writer in favor of making a reasonable living for himself as a writer of boys' books to supplement his income as a minister.

After ministering to the Brewster church for just fifteen months, Alger was suddenly dismissed from his post for "gross immorality and a most heinous crime." The offense, as described in a church report sent to the American Unitarian Association office in Boston, was "a crime of no less magnitude than the abominable and revolting crime of unnatural familiarity with *boys*." Alger did not contest the charges made by two boys in the church; he left Brewster quickly before he could be arrested or possibly attacked by members of the enraged community. After he sent a letter to the Association explaining that he was resigning for reasons of health and requesting that the church handle the matter discreetly because he promised never again to seek a ministry, he headed for New York City and the shelter of anonymity it offered. He managed to keep the incident a secret throughout his life, and it remained so for more than a hundred years.

In New York he devoted himself to writing books that would serve as models of behavior for the abandoned boys he observed in the streets. He would spend the next thirty years in New York writing for them, because he felt, as he put it, "called" to helping them to help themselves. He didn't write stories about individual boys so much as he wrote about a class of boys whose lives he believed could be made better if they were made aware of their own possibilities. These could be achieved through individual effort, self-discipline, and a conscious application of virtue. However complicated and problematic Alger's own life was (there is no evidence available to indicate that he ever had any further sexual encounters with boys), he made the path to success as straightforward as possible for his boys.

Alger's plots are decidedly generic and lend themselves to formulaic summaries. Despite their numbers, his novels pretty much conform to a proven recipe that did not experiment with the tastes of his readers. Instead, he fed them what they had already demonstrated an appetite for in their choice of reading. Describing a typical Alger plot is a necessary reduction of the novel's ingredients, but the process does not spoil the book's flavor. Because Alger occasionally signed autographs by blending together titles of his own books, his cue is an appropriate means to describe the stories' characters, conflicts, and plots. Here is a boilerplate for the typical "Horatio Alger story" culled from his titles: Perilously *Adrift in the City* with *The Odds Against Him* but *The World Before Him,* a *Brave and Bold* poor boy of about fifteen years old is *Driven from Home* and, *Shifting for Himself,* sets out to *Strive and Succeed* by *Struggling Upward* and *Forging Ahead. Facing the World* with *Grit* and a *Rough and Ready* honest good nature, he overcomes the social corruption swirling around him because he understands that *A Boy's Fortune* is built upon manly virtue. Though his father is dead, his faithful mother has taught him to *Wait and Hope.* Knowing he must *Sink or Swim* to avoid being *Cast upon the Breakers,* his *Do and Dare,* as well as his *Luck and Pluck,* assist him in *Making His Way* and in looking *Out for Business. Seeking His Fortune,* this *Strong and Steady* lad moves *Up the Ladder,* because he is not afraid to *Try and Trust.* Unlike his selfish or snobbish rivals who smoke, drink, or gamble, the hero is *Bound to Rise,* since he learns to live clean and neither cheats nor lies. Never one to avoid a *Debt of Honor,* he rescues a rich man's child or returns a rich man's wallet, thus *Making His Mark* forthrightly *In a New World.* Thereafter, though his progress may be *Slow and Sure,* he knows that he can *Wait and Win.* By *Helping Himself* he is, at the end of the story, inevitably *Risen from the Ranks* and eager to help others.

If you've read one of these novels, you haven't read them all, but there are few surprises along the way. Whether the hero's name is Tattered Tom, Mark the Match Boy, Paul the Peddler, Luke Larkin, Nelson the Newsboy, or Ragged Dick, the protagonists' actions repeatedly depict basically the same plot, and that's the story Alger was sticking with through scores of novels. His readers were not bothered by the predictable repetitive nature of his plots. Like most consumers of formula fiction, Alger's audience found his stories emotionally satisfying because his readers were secure in their expectations; their heroes' success allowed them to feel safe in a competitive world that was otherwise intimidating and frightening.

In *Ragged Dick; or, Street Life in New York with the Boot Blacks,* the titular hero, Dick Hunter, starts off as a homeless fourteen-year-old bootblack who is orphaned and has been on his own since he was seven. In spite of his filthy torn clothes and the streaks of dirt covering his face and hands, "there was something about Dick that was attractive" (p. 4). He is direct and unapologetic, and is made handsome by his "energy, ambition, and natural sharpness," qualities that make him "distinguished" (p. 168) in comparison to other street urchins. His strong character causes street thugs to envy him while it prompts successful gentlemen to recognize his potential and want to help him. These appealing qualities also allowed Alger's readers to identify with Dick even though he complains early in the story that reading gives him a headache, because he really doesn't know how to read. Dick becomes the perfect consumer model for the book when his avuncular patron, Mr. Whitney, urges him to understand that "in this free country poverty in early life is no bar to a man's advancement. . . . Save your money, my lad, buy books, and determine to be somebody" (pp. 71–72).

Like Dick, who learns to read and saves his money for books, readers eagerly did buy into Alger's story. The novel first appeared in serial form in the 1867 issues of *Student and Schoolmaster,* a monthly juvenile magazine. Because the serial was so popular, Alger revised and expanded it for book publication in 1868, when it became the bestselling book of his entire career, and which he described in its preface as "the first volume of a series intended to illustrate the life and experiences of the friendless and vagrant children who are now numbered by thousands in New York and other cities" (p. 1).

The book was praised by reviewers for its inspirational value for young boys, and Alger was applauded for his philanthropic efforts to portray street boys sympathetically and insightfully. This success led to five more novels in the Ragged Dick series, which charted the steady upward course of a variety of hardworking, deserving street boys.

While Alger's boy readers were not troubled by the lack of variety in his plots or the deficiencies in his writing style, his adult readers also looked past his fast shoddy writing in exchange for the inspirational characters he encouraged his audiences to dream themselves into. If a prosperous gentleman happened to have a child who required rescuing and would reward Ragged Dick for his heroic deed by helping him secure a respectable job, that remarkable coincidence (one of many) was all right with them. Because Alger often had to write quickly—he had almost as much difficulty making a living as the bootblacks he described—he would sometimes lose track of a character's name or include contradictory information about what a character said or did. Whether from forgetfulness or a need to fill up a page, he retold points that had already been repeated at other moments in the story. Dick, for instance, is "an enterprising young man" (p. 19) who is "always . . . ready for business" (p. 7), "always" with "an eye to business" (p. 14).

This absentmindedness is less noticeable, however, than Alger's stilted language and mind-numbing descriptions. Consider, for example, this report of Dick and a friend touring part of the city:

> The Sixth Avenue is lined with stores, many of them of very good appearance, and would make a very respectable principal street for a good-sized city. But it is only one of several long business streets which run up the island, and illustrate the extent and importance of the city to which they belong.

No incidents worth mentioning took place during
their ride down town.   (p. 63)

Or consider the narrator's moralistic and dour digression
about smoking: "No boy of fourteen can smoke without being affected injuriously. Men are frequently injured by
smoking, and boys always" (p. 7). The pace is also slowed
by wooden dialogue as when Dick's friend Frank asks him a
question (which ends with a question mark) and Alger tacks
on this: "said Frank, interrogatively" (p. 40).

Although twenty-first-century readers may find Alger's
style amusing as well as inept, it would be a mistake to write
off what was appealing in the novels to his contemporary
readers. They were not, after all, engaged in a comparative
analysis of Alger's style with that of, say, Henry James or
Mark Twain. They read the novels for their straightforward
portrayals of characters that could readily be identified as
good or bad and for the wholesome lessons presented in
simple language that might help them to negotiate their own
struggles.

The moral clarity in Alger's novels provided an antidote
to the poverty, disease, and crime in New York's slums. That
world was vividly described by Charles Loring Brace, who
in 1853 established the Children's Aid Society in response
to the deplorable conditions he later evoked in *The Dangerous Classes of New York* (1872):

the young ruffians of New York are one of the products
of accident, ignorance, and vice. Among a million people, such as compose the population of this city and its
suburbs, there will always be a great number of misfor-
tunes: fathers die, and leave their children unprovided
for; parents drink, and abuse their little ones, and they
float away on the currents of the street; step-mothers or
step-fathers drive out, by neglect and ill-treatment, their

sons from home. Thousands are the children of poor
foreigners, who have permitted them to grow up without school, education, or religion. All the neglect and
bad education and evil example of the poor class tend
to form others, who, as they mature, swell the ranks of
ruffians and criminals. So, at length, a great multitude
of ignorant, untrained passionate, irreligious boys and
young men are formed, who become the "dangerous
class" of our city. They form . . . the young burglers
and murderers, the garroters and rioters, the thieves
and flash-men, the "repeaters" and ruffians, so well
known to all who know this metropolis.

These "street-rats," as they were called by the police,
were treated by Alger not as infestations but as boys who
could be redeemed by being shown exemplary models rather
than the back of someone's hand. He knew from experience
how difficult street life was for them owing to his involve-
ment with the Children's Aid Society and the Newsboys
Lodging House. He supported these philanthropic missions
because they offered clean beds and clear values to homeless boys from the worst neighborhoods who had nowhere to
turn. His novels were reformist attempts to alert them to the
dangerous and chaotic nature of urban life—a city crammed
with pickpockets, swindlers, con men, dissemblers, liars,
drunks, and the brutality of crushing poverty. Although Alger does not depict the violence and prostituted lives of
street life in the gritty realistic manner that, for example,
Stephen Crane would later portray in *Maggie, A Girl of the
Streets* (1893), his more genteel treatment nevertheless inti-
mates the dangers awaiting the uninitiated and the unsus-
pecting. His stories focused on how to animate his readers'
latent virtues rather than on rehearsing the miserable details
of their lives. Not surprisingly, the very first words of *Ragged Dick* are "Wake up there, youngster" (p. 3).

Alger's novels were purposely formulaic: they were recipes, prescriptions, directions, instructions, and manuals that taught by example, one plot after the next, how to survive a world that conspired against the hopes, the desires, and the most fundamental needs of their protagonists. As Dick warns, "A feller has to look sharp in this city, or he'll lose his eye-teeth before he knows it" (p. 66). Despite the corny dialogue and the traditional lessons about middle-class manners and morals, there is a kind of feral shrewdness inherent in some of Alger's heroes that is masked by their "drollery" and cheery dispositions. Dick Hunter smiles a lot, but a careful reader will also notice that he guards and retains his canines.

For contemporary readers who are more than a little wary and skeptical of the benevolence of American business practices, corporate values, and employer loyalties, the respectability that Dick achieves at the novel's end may seem like the beginning of a cruel joke. If Dick's prospects of "fame and fortune" seem merely nostalgic and improbable, his actual principles—honesty, hard work, conscientiousness, hopeful expectations, and charity—are not. To laugh at those values, to dismiss them as naive, unworldly, and simple-minded, is to spurn genuine virtue and to wink at the rapacious villains of the piece who are the cheats, liars, and unscrupulous manipulators. His villains may seem more credible, but Alger's heroes are worth remembering even if his readers are chastened by history.

—Michael Meyer

Preface

"RAGGED DICK" was contributed as a serial story to the pages of the SCHOOLMATE, a well-known juvenile magazine, during the year 1867. While in course of publication, it was received with so many evidences of favor that it has been rewritten and considerably enlarged, and is now presented to the public as the first volume of a series intended to illustrate the life and experiences of the friendless and vagrant children who are now numbered by thousands in New York and other cities.

Several characters in the story are sketched from life. The necessary information has been gathered mainly from personal observation and conversations with the boys themselves. The author is indebted also to the excellent Superintendent of the Newsboys' Lodging House, in Fulton Street, for some facts of which he has been able to make use. Some anachronisms may be noted. Wherever they occur, they have been admitted, as aiding in the development of the story, and will probably be considered as of little importance in an unpretending volume, which does not aspire to strict historical accuracy.

The author hopes that, while the volumes in this series may prove interesting as stories, they may also have the effect of enlisting the sympathies of his readers in behalf of the unfortunate children whose life is described, and of leading them to co-operate with the praiseworthy efforts now making [sic] by the Children's Aid Society and other organizations to ameliorate their condition.

New York, April, 1868

CHAPTER I

Ragged Dick Is Introduced to the Reader

"WAKE up there, youngster," said a rough voice.

Ragged Dick opened his eyes slowly, and stared stupidly in the face of the speaker, but did not offer to get up.

"Wake up, you young vagabond!" said the man a little impatiently; "I suppose you'd lay there all day, if I hadn't called you."

"What time is it?" asked Dick.

"Seven o'clock."

"Seven o'clock! I oughter 've been up an hour ago. I know what 'twas made me so precious sleepy. I went to the Old Bowery last night, and didn't turn in till past twelve."

"You went to the Old Bowery? Where'd you get your money?" asked the man, who was a porter in the employ of a firm doing business on Spruce Street.

"Made it by shines, in course. My guardian don't allow me no money for theatres, so I have to earn it."

"Some boys get it easier than that," said the porter significantly.

"You don't catch me stealin', if that's what you mean," said Dick.

"Don't you ever steal, then?"

"No, and I wouldn't. Lots of boys does it, but I wouldn't."

"Well, I'm glad to hear you say that. I believe there's some good in you, Dick, after all."

"Oh, I'm a rough customer!" said Dick. "But I wouldn't steal. It's mean."

"I'm glad you think so, Dick," and the rough voice sounded gentler than at first. "Have you got any money to buy your breakfast?"

"No, but I'll soon get some."

While this conversation has been going on, Dick had got up. His bedchamber had been a wooden box half full of straw, on which the young boot-black had reposed his weary limbs, and slept as soundly as if it had been a bed of down. He dumped down into the straw without taking the trouble of undressing. Getting up too was an equally short process. He jumped out of the box, shook himself, picked out one or two straws that had found their way into rents in his clothes, and, drawing a well-worn cap over his uncombed locks, he was all ready for the business of the day.

Dick's appearance as he stood beside the box was rather peculiar. His pants were torn in several places, and had apparently belonged in the first instance to a boy two sizes larger than himself. He wore a vest, all the buttons of which were gone except two, out of which peeped a shirt which looked as if it had been worn a month. To complete his costume he wore a coat too long for him, dating back, if one might judge from its general appearance, to a remote antiquity.

Washing the face and hands is usually considered proper in commencing the day, but Dick was above such refinement. He had no particular dislike to dirt, and did not think it necessary to remove several dark streaks on his face and hands. But in spite of his dirt and rags there was something about Dick that was attractive. It was easy to see that if he

had been clean and well dressed he would have been decidedly good-looking. Some of his companions were sly, and
their faces inspired distrust; but Dick had a frank, straight-
forward manner that made him a favorite.

Dick's business hours had commenced. He had no office
to open. His little blacking-box was ready for use, and he
looked sharply in the faces of all who passed, addressing
each with, "Shine yer boots, sir?"

"How much?" asked a gentleman on his way to his office.

"Ten cents," said Dick, dropping his box, and sinking
upon his knees on the sidewalk, flourishing his brush with
the air of one skilled in his profession.

"Ten cents! Isn't that a little steep?"

"Well, you know 'taint all clear profit," said Dick, who
had already set to work. "There's the *blacking* costs something, and I have to get a new brush pretty often."

"And you have a large rent too," said the gentleman quiz-
zically, with a glance at a large hole in Dick's coat.

"Yes, sir," said Dick, always ready to joke; "I have to pay
such a big rent for my manshun up on Fifth Avenoo, that I
can't afford to take less than ten cents a shine. I'll give you a
bully shine, sir."

"Be quick about it, for I am in a hurry. So your house is
on Fifth Avenue, is it?"

"It isn't anywhere else," said Dick, and Dick spoke the
truth there.

"What tailor do you patronize?" asked the gentleman,
surveying Dick's attire.

"Would you like to go to the same one?" asked Dick,
shrewdly.

"Well, no; it strikes me that he didn't give you a very
good fit."

"This coat once belonged to General Washington," said
Dick, comically. "He wore it all through the Revolution, and
it got torn some, 'cause he fit so hard. When he died he told

his widder to give it to some smart young feller that hadn't got none of his own; so she gave it to me. But if you'd like it, sir, to remember General Washington by, I'll let you have it reasonable."

"Thank you, but I wouldn't want to deprive you of it. And did your pants come from General Washington too?"

"No, they was a gift from Lewis Napoleon. Lewis had outgrown 'em and sent 'em to me,—he's bigger than me, and that's why they don't fit."

"It seems you have distinguished friends. Now, my lad, I suppose you would like your money."

"I shouldn't have any objection," said Dick.

"I believe," said the gentleman, examining his pocket-book, "I haven't got anything short of twenty-five cents. Have you got any change?"

"Not a cent," said Dick. "All my money's invested in the Erie Railroad."

"That's unfortunate."

"Shall I get the money changed, sir?"

"I can't wait; I've got to meet an appointment immediately. I'll hand you twenty-five cents, and you can leave the change at my office any time during the day."

"All right, sir. Where is it?"

"No. 125 Fulton Street. Shall you remember?"

"Yes, sir. What name?"

"Greyson—office on second floor."

"All right, sir; I'll bring it."

"I wonder whether the little scamp will prove honest," said Mr. Greyson to himself, as he walked away. "If he does, I'll give him my custom regularly. If he don't, as is most likely, I shan't mind the loss of fifteen cents."

Mr. Greyson didn't understand Dick. Our ragged hero wasn't a model boy in all respects. I am afraid he swore sometimes, and now and then he played tricks upon unsophisticated boys from the country, or gave a wrong direction to honest old gentlemen unused to the city. A clergyman in search of the Cooper Institute he once directed to the Tombs Prison, and, following him unobserved, was highly delighted when the unsuspicious stranger walked up the front steps of the great stone building on Centre Street, and tried to obtain admission.

"I guess he wouldn't want to stay long if he did get in," thought Ragged Dick, hitching up his pants. "Leastways I shouldn't. They're so precious glad to see you that they won't let you go, but board you gratooitous, and never send in no bills."

Another of Dick's faults was his extravagance. Being always wide-awake and ready for business, he earned enough to have supported him comfortably and respectably. There were not a few young clerks who employed Dick from time to time in his professional capacity, who scarcely earned as much as he, greatly as their style and dress exceeded his. But Dick was careless of his earnings. Where they went he could hardly have told himself. However much he managed to earn during the day, all was generally spent before morning. He was fond of going to the Old Bowery Theatre, and to Tony Pastor's, and if he had any money left afterwards, he would invite some of his friends in somewhere to have an oyster stew; so it seldom happened that he commenced the day with a penny.

Then I am sorry to add that Dick had formed the habit of smoking. This cost him considerable, for Dick was rather fastidious about his cigars, and wouldn't smoke the cheapest. Besides, having a liberal nature, he was generally ready to treat his companions. But of course the expense was the smallest objection. No boy of fourteen can smoke without being affected injuriously. Men are frequently injured by smoking, and boys always. But large numbers of the newsboys and boot-blacks form the habit. Exposed to the cold and wet they find that it warms them up, and the self-indulgence grows upon them. It is not uncommon to see a little boy, too young to be out of his mother's sight, smoking with all the apparent satisfaction of a veteran smoker.

There was another way in which Dick sometimes lost money. There was a noted gambling-house on Baxter Street, which in the evening was sometimes crowded with these juvenile gamesters, who staked their hard earnings, generally losing of course, and refreshing themselves from time to time with a vile mixture of liquor at two cents a glass. Sometimes Dick strayed in here, and played with the rest.

I have mentioned Dick's faults and defects, because I want it understood, to begin with, that I don't consider him a model boy. But there were some good points about him nevertheless. He was above doing anything mean or dishonorable. He would not steal, or cheat, or impose upon younger boys, but was frank and straight-forward, manly and self-reliant. His nature was a noble one, and had saved him from all mean faults. I hope my young readers will like him as I do, without being blind to his faults. Perhaps, although he was only a boot-black, they may find something in him to imitate.

And now, having fairly introduced Ragged Dick to my young readers, I must refer them to the next chapter for his further adventures.

CHAPTER II

Johnny Nolan

AFTER Dick had finished polishing Mr. Greyson's boots he was fortunate enough to secure three other customers, two of them reporters in the Tribune establishment, which occupies the corner of Spruce Street and Printing House Square.

When Dick had got through with his last customer the City Hall clock indicated eight o'clock. He had been up an hour, and hard at work, and naturally began to think of breakfast. He went up to the head of Spruce Street, and turned into Nassau. Two blocks further, and he reached Ann Street. On this street was a small, cheap restaurant, where for five cents Dick could get a cup of coffee, and for ten cents more, a plate of beefsteak with a plate of bread thrown in. These Dick ordered, and sat down at a table.

It was a small apartment with a few plain tables unprovided with cloths, for the class of customers who patronized it were not very particular. Our hero's breakfast was soon before him. Neither the coffee nor the steak were as good as can be bought at Delmonico's; but then it is very doubtful whether, in the present state of his wardrobe, Dick would have been received at that aristocratic restaurant, even if his means had admitted of paying the high prices there charged.

Dick had scarcely been served when he espied a boy about his own size standing at the door, looking wistfully into the restaurant. This was Johnny Nolan, a boy of fourteen, who was engaged in the same profession as Ragged Dick. His wardrobe was in very much the same condition as Dick's.

"Had your breakfast, Johnny?" inquired Dick, cutting off a piece of steak.

"No."

"Come in, then. Here's room for you."

"I ain't got no money," said Johnny, looking a little enviously at his more fortunate friend.

"Haven't you had any shines?"

"Yes, I had one, but I shan't get any pay till to-morrow."

"Are you hungry?"

"Try me, and see."

"Come in. I'll stand treat this morning."

Johnny Nolan was nowise slow to accept this invitation, and was soon seated beside Dick.

"What'll you have, Johnny?"

"Same as you."

"Cup o' coffee and beefsteak," ordered Dick.

These were promptly brought, and Johnny attacked them vigorously.

Now, in the boot-blacking business, as well as in higher avocations, the same rule prevails, that energy and industry are rewarded, and indolence suffers. Dick was energetic and on the alert for business, but Johnny the reverse. The consequence was that Dick earned probably three times as much as the other.

"How do you like it?" asked Dick, surveying Johnny's attacks upon the steak with evident complacency.

"It's hunky."

I don't believe "hunky" is to be found in either Webster's or Worcester's big dictionary; but boys will readily understand what it means.

"Do you come here often?" asked Johnny.

"Most every day. You'd better come too."

"I can't afford it."

"Well, you'd ought to, then," said Dick. "What do you do with your money, I'd like to know?"

"I don't get near as much as you, Dick."

"Well, you might if you tried. I keep my eyes open—that's the way I get jobs. You're lazy, that's what's the matter."

Johnny did not see fit to reply to this charge. Probably he felt the justice of it, and preferred to proceed with the breakfast, which he enjoyed the more as it cost him nothing.

Breakfast over, Dick walked up to the desk, and settled the bill. Then, followed by Johnny, he went out into the street.

"Where are you going, Johnny?"

"Up to Mr. Taylor's, on Spruce Street, to see if he don't want a shine."

"Do you work for him reg'lar?"

"Yes. Him and his partner wants a shine most every day. Where are you goin'?"

"Down front of the Astor House. I guess I'll find some customers there."

At this moment Johnny started, and, dodging into an entry way, hid behind the door, considerably to Dick's surprise.

"What's the matter now?" asked our hero.

"Has he gone?" asked Johnny, his voice betraying anxiety.

"Who gone, I'd like to know?"

"That man in the brown coat."

"What of him. You ain't scared of him, are you?"

"Yes, he got me a place once."

"Where?"

"Ever so far off."

"What if he did?"

"I ran away."

"Didn't you like it?"

"No, I had to get up too early. It was on a farm, and I had to get up at five to take care of the cows. I like New York best."

"Didn't they give you enough to eat?"

"Oh, yes, plenty."

"And you had a good bed?"

"Yes."

"Then you'd better have stayed. You don't get either of them here. Where'd you sleep last night?"

"Up an alley in an old wagon."

"You had a better bed than that in the country, didn't you?"

"Yes, it was as soft as—as cotton."

Johnny had once slept on a bale of cotton, the recollection supplying him with a comparison.

"Why didn't you stay?"

"I felt lonely," said Johnny.

Johnny could not exactly explain his feelings, but it is often the case that the young vagabond of the streets, though his food is uncertain, and his bed may be any old wagon or barrel that he is lucky enough to find unoccupied when night sets in, gets so attached to his precarious but independent mode of life, that he feels discontented in any other. He is accustomed to the noise and bustle and ever-varied life of the streets, and in the quiet scenes of the country misses the excitement in the midst of which he has always dwelt.

Johnny had but one tie to bind him to the city. He had a father living, but he might as well have been without one. Mr. Nolan was a confirmed drunkard, and spent the greater part of his wages for liquor. His potations made him ugly, and in-

flamed a temper never very sweet, working him up sometimes to such a pitch of rage that Johnny's life was in danger.
Some months before, he had thrown a flat-iron at his son's
head with such terrific force that unless Johnny had dodged
he would not have lived long enough to obtain a place in our
story. He fled the house, and from that time had not dared to
re-enter it. Somebody had given him a brush and box of
blacking, and he had set up in business on his own account.
But he had not energy enough to succeed, as has already been
stated, and I am afraid the poor boy had met with many hard-
ships, and suffered more than once from cold and hunger.
Dick had befriended him more than once, and often given
him a breakfast or dinner, as the case might be.

"How'd you get away?" asked Dick, with some curiosity.
"Did you walk?"

"No, I rode on the cars."

"Where'd you get your money? I hope you didn't steal it."

"I didn't have none."

"What did you do, then?"

"I got up about three o'clock, and walked to Albany."

"Where's that?" asked Dick, whose ideas on the subject
of geography were rather vague.

"Up the river."

"How far?"

"About a thousand miles," said Johnny, whose concep-
tions of distance were equally vague.

"Go ahead. What did you do then?"

"I hid on top of a freight car, and came all the way without their seeing me.* That man in the brown coat was the
man that got me the place, and I'm afraid he'd want to send
me back."

"Well," said Dick, reflectively, "I dunno as I'd like to live
in the country. I couldn't go to Tony Pastor's, or the Old

* A fact.

Bowery. There wouldn't be no place to spend my evenings. But I say, it's tough in winter, Johnny, 'specially when your overcoat's at the tailor's, an' likely to stay there."

"That's so, Dick. But I must be goin', or Mr. Taylor'll get somebody else to shine his boots."

Johnny walked back to Nassau Street, while Dick kept on his way to Broadway.

"That boy," soliloquized Dick, as Johnny took his departure, "ain't got no ambition. I'll bet he won't get five shines to-day. I'm glad I ain't like him. I couldn't go to the theatre, nor buy no cigars, nor get half as much as I wanted to eat.— Shine yer boots, sir?"

Dick always had an eye to business, and this remark was addressed to a young man, dressed in a stylish manner, who was swinging a jaunty cane.

"I've had my boots blacked once already this morning, but this confounded mud has spoiled the shine."

"I'll make 'em all right, sir, in a minute."

"Go ahead, then."

The boots were soon polished in Dick's best style, which proved very satisfactory, our hero being a proficient in the art.

"I haven't got any change," said the young man, fumbling in his pocket, "but here's a bill you may run somewhere and get changed. I'll pay you five cents extra for your trouble."

He handed Dick a two-dollar bill, which our hero took into a store close by.

"Will you please change that, sir?" said Dick, walking up to the counter.

The salesman to whom he proffered it took the bill, and, slightly glancing at it, exclaimed angrily, "Be off, you young vagabond, or I'll have you arrested."

"What's the row?"

"You've offered me a counterfeit bill."

"I didn't know it," said Dick.

"Don't tell me. Be off, or I'll have you arrested."

CHAPTER III

Dick Makes a Proposition

THOUGH Dick was somewhat startled at discovering that the bill he had offered was counterfeit, he stood his ground bravely.

"Clear out of this shop, you young vagabond," repeated the clerk.

"Then give me back my bill."

"That you may pass it again? No, sir, I shall do no such thing."

"It doesn't belong to me," said Dick. "A gentleman that owes me for a shine gave it to me to change."

"A likely story," said the clerk; but he seemed a little uneasy.

"I'll go and call him," said Dick.

He went out, and found his late customer standing on the Astor House steps.

"Well, youngster, have you brought back my change? You were a precious long time about it. I began to think you had cleared out with the money."

"That ain't my style," said Dick, proudly.

"Then where's the change?"

"I haven't got it."

"Where's the bill then?"

"I haven't got that either."

"You young rascal!"

"Hold on a minute, mister," said Dick, "and I'll tell you all about it. The man what took the bill said it wasn't good, and kept it."

"The bill was perfectly good. So he kept it, did he? I'll go with you to the store, and see whether he won't give it back to me."

Dick led the way, and the gentleman followed him into the store. At the reappearance of Dick in such company, the clerk flushed a little, and looked nervous. He fancied that he could browbeat a ragged boot-black, but with a gentleman he saw that it would be a different matter. He did not seem to notice the new-comers, but began to replace some goods on the shelves.

"Now," said the young man, "point out the clerk that has my money."

"That's him," said Dick, pointing out the clerk.

The gentleman walked up to the counter.

"I will trouble you," he said a little haughtily, "for a bill which that boy offered you, and which you still hold in your possession."

"It was a bad bill," said the clerk, his cheek flushing, and his manner nervous.

"It was no such thing. I require you to produce it, and let the matter be decided."

The clerk fumbled in his vest-pocket, and drew out a bad-looking bill.

"This is a bad bill, but it is not the one I gave the boy."

"It is the one he gave me."

The young man looked doubtful.

"Boy," he said to Dick, "is this the bill you gave to be changed?"

"No, it isn't."

"You lie, you young rascal!" exclaimed the clerk, who began to find himself in a tight place, and could not see the way out.

This scene naturally attracted the attention of all in the store, and the proprietor walked up from the lower end, where he had been busy

"What's all this, Mr. Hatch?" he demanded.

"That boy," said the clerk, "came in and asked change for a bad bill. I kept the bill, and told him to clear out. Now he wants it again to pass on somebody else."

"Show the bill."

The merchant looked at it. "Yes, that's a bad bill," he said. "There is no doubt about that."

"But it is not the one the boy offered," said Dick's patron. "It is one of the same denomination, but on a different bank."

"Do you remember what bank it was on?"

"It was on the Merchants' Bank of Boston."

"Are you sure of it?"

"I am."

"Perhaps the boy kept it and offered the other."

"You may search me if you want to," said Dick, indignantly.

"He doesn't look as if he was likely to have any extra bills. I suspect that your clerk pocketed the good bill, and has substituted the counterfeit note. It is a nice little scheme of his for making money."

"I haven't seen any bill on the Merchants' Bank," said the clerk, doggedly.

"You had better feel in your pockets."

"This matter must be investigated," said the merchant, firmly. "If you have the bill, produce it."

"I haven't got it," said the clerk; but he looked guilty notwithstanding.

"I demand that he be searched," said Dick's patron.

"I tell you I haven't got it."

"Shall I send for a police officer, Mr. Hatch, or will you allow yourself to be searched quietly?" said the merchant.

Alarmed at the threat implied in these words, the clerk put his hand into his vest-pocket, and drew out a two-dollar bill on the Merchants' Bank.

"Is this your note?" asked the shopkeeper, showing it to the young man.

"It is."

"I must have made a mistake," faltered the clerk.

"I shall not give you a chance to make such another mistake in my employ," said the merchant sternly. "You may go up to the desk and ask for what wages are due you. I shall have no further occasion for your services."

"Now, youngster," said Dick's patron, as they went out of the store, after he had finally got the bill changed. "I must pay you something extra for your trouble. Here's fifty cents."

"Thank you, sir," said Dick. "You're very kind. Don't you want some more bills changed?"

"Not to-day," said he with a smile. "It's too expensive."

"I'm in luck," thought our hero complacently. "I guess I'll go to Barnum's to-night, and see the bearded lady, the eight-foot giant, the two-foot dwarf, and the other curiosities, too numerous to mention."

Dick shouldered his box and walked up as far as the Astor House. He took his station on the sidewalk, and began to look about him.

Just behind him were two persons,—one, a gentleman of fifty; the other, a boy of thirteen or fourteen. They were speaking together, and Dick had no difficulty in hearing what was said.

"I am sorry, Frank, that I can't go about, and show you some of the sights of New York, but I shall be full of business to-day. It is your first visit to the city too."

"Yes, sir."

"There's a good deal worth seeing here. But I'm afraid you'll have to wait till next time. You can go out and walk by yourself, but don't venture too far, or you may get lost."

Frank looked disappointed.

"I wish Tom Miles knew I was here," he said. "He would go around with me."

"Where does he live?"

"Somewhere up town, I believe."

"Then, unfortunately, he is not available. If you would rather go with me than stay here, you can, but as I shall be most of the time in merchants' counting-rooms, I am afraid it would not be very interesting."

"I think," said Frank, after a little hesitation, "that I will go off by myself. I won't go very far, and if I lose my way, I will inquire for the Astor House."

"Yes, anybody will direct you here."

"Very well, Frank, I am sorry I can't do better for you. Oh, never mind, uncle, I shall be amused in walking around, and looking at the shop-windows. There will be a great deal to see."

Now Dick had listened to all this conversation. Being an enterprising young man, he thought he saw a chance for a speculation, and determined to avail himself of it.

Accordingly he stepped up to the two just as Frank's uncle was about leaving, and said, "I know all about the city, sir; I'll show him around, if you want me to."

The gentleman looked a little curiously at the ragged figure before him.

"So you are a city boy, are you?"

"Yes, sir," said Dick, "I've lived here ever since I was a baby."

"And you know all about the public buildings, I suppose?"

"Yes, sir."

"And the Central Park?"

"Yes, sir. I know my way all round."

The gentleman looked thoughtful.

"I don't know what to say, Frank," he remarked after a while. "It is rather a novel proposal. He isn't exactly the sort of guide I would have picked out for you. Still he looks honest. He has an open face, and I think can be depended upon."

"I wish he wasn't so ragged and dirty," said Frank, who felt a little shy about being seen with such a companion.

"I'm afraid you haven't washed your face this morning," said Mr. Whitney, for that was the gentleman's name.

"They didn't have no wash-bowls at the hotel where I stopped," said Dick.

"What hotel did you stop at?"

"The Box Hotel."

"The Box Hotel?"

"Yes, sir, I slept in a box on Spruce Street."

Frank surveyed Dick curiously.

"How did you like it?" he asked.

"I slept bully."

"Suppose it had rained."

"Then I'd have wet my best clothes," said Dick.

"Are these all the clothes you have?"

"Yes, sir."

Mr. Whitney spoke a few words to Frank, who seemed pleased with the suggestion.

"Follow me, my lad," he said.

Dick in some surprise obeyed orders, following Mr. Whitney and Frank into the hotel, past the office, to the foot of the staircase. Here a servant of the hotel stopped Dick, but Mr. Whitney explained that he had something for him to do, and he was allowed to proceed.

They entered a long entry, and finally paused before a door. This being opened a pleasant chamber was disclosed.

"Come in, my lad," said Mr. Whitney

Dick and Frank entered.

CHAPTER IV

Dick's New Suit

"Now," said Mr. Whitney to Dick, "my nephew here is on his way to a boarding-school. He had a suit of clothes in his trunk about half worn. He is willing to give them to you. I think they will look better than those you have on."

Dick was so astonished that he hardly knew what to say. Presents were something that he knew very little about, never having received any to his knowledge. That so large a gift should be made to him by a stranger seemed very wonderful.

The clothes were brought out, and turned out to be a neat gray suit.

"Before you put them on, my lad, you must wash yourself. Clean clothes and a dirty skin don't go very well together. Frank, you may attend to him. I am obliged to go at once. Have you got as much money as you require?"

"Yes, uncle."

"One more word, my lad," said Mr. Whitney, addressing Dick; "I may be rash in trusting a boy of whom I know nothing, but I like your looks, and I think you will prove a proper guide for my nephew."

"Yes, I will, sir," said Dick, earnestly. "Honor bright!"

"Very well. A pleasant time to you."

The process of cleansing commenced. To tell the truth Dick needed it, and the sensation of cleanliness he found both new and pleasant. Frank added to his gift a shirt, stockings, and an old pair of shoes. "I am sorry I haven't any cap," said he.

"I've got one," said Dick.

"It isn't so new as it might be," said Frank, surveying an old felt hat, which had once been black, but was now dingy, with a large hole in the top and a portion of the rim torn off.

"No," said Dick; "my grandfather used to wear it when he was a boy, and I've kep' it ever since out of respect for his memory. But I'll get a new one now. I can buy one cheap on Chatham Street."

"Is that near here?"

"Only five minutes' walk."

"Then we can get it on the way."

When Dick was dressed in his new attire, with his face and hands clean, and his hair brushed, it was difficult to imagine that he was the same boy.

He now looked quite handsome, and might readily have been taken for a young gentleman, except that his hands were red and grimy.

"Look at yourself," said Frank, leading him before the mirror.

"By gracious!" said Dick, starting back in astonishment, "that isn't me, is it?"

"Don't you know yourself?" asked Frank, smiling.

"It reminds me of Cinderella," said Dick, "when she was changed into a fairy princess. I see it one night at Barnum's. What'll Johnny Nolan say when he sees me? He won't dare to speak to such a young swell as I be now. Ain't it rich?" and Dick burst into a loud laugh. His fancy was tickled by the anticipation of his friend's surprise. Then the thought of the valuable gifts he had received occurred to him, and he looked gratefully at Frank.

"You're a brick," he said.

"A what?"

"A brick! You're a jolly good fellow to give me such a present."

"You're quite welcome, Dick," said Frank, kindly. "I'm better off than you are, and I can spare the clothes just as well as not. You must have a new hat though. But that we can get when we go out. The old clothes you can make into a bundle."

"Wait a minute till I get my handkercher," and Dick pulled from the pocket of the pants a dirty rag, which might have been white once, though it did not look like it, and had apparently once formed a part of a sheet or shirt.

"You mustn't carry that," said Frank.

"But I've got a cold," said Dick.

"Oh, I don't mean you to go without a handkerchief. I'll give you one."

Frank opened his trunk and pulled out two, which he gave to Dick.

"I wonder if I ain't dreamin'," said Dick, once more surveying himself doubtfully in the glass. "I'm afraid I'm dreamin', and shall wake up in a barrel, as I did night afore last."

"Shall I pinch you so you can wake here?" asked Frank, playfully.

"Yes," said Dick, seriously, "I wish you would."

He pulled up the sleeve of his jacket, and Frank pinched him pretty hard, so that Dick winced.

"Yes, I guess I'm awake," said Dick; "you've got a pair of nippers, you have.

"But what shall I do with my brush and blacking?" he asked.

"You can leave them here till we come back," said Frank. "They will be safe."

"Hold on a minute," said Dick, surveying Frank's boots with a professional eye, "you ain't got a good shine on them boots. I'll make 'em shine so you can see your face in 'em."

And he was as good as his word.

"Thank you," said Frank; "now you had better brush your own shoes."

This had not occurred to Dick, for in general the professional boot-black considers his blacking too valuable to expend on his own shoes or boots, if he is fortunate enough to possess a pair.

The two boys now went downstairs together. They met the same servant who had spoken to Dick a few minutes before, but there was no recognition.

"He don't know me," said Dick. "He thinks I'm a young swell like you."

"What's a swell?"

"Oh, a feller that wears nobby clothes like you."

"And you, too, Dick."

"Yes," said Dick, "who'd ever have thought as I should have turned into a swell?"

They had now got out on Broadway, and were slowly walking along the west side by the Park, when who should Dick see in front of him, but Johnny Nolan?

Instantly Dick was seized with a fancy for witnessing Johnny's amazement at his change in appearance. He stole up behind him, and struck him on the back.

"Hallo, Johnny, how many shines have you had?"

Johnny turned round expecting to see Dick, whose voice he recognized, but his astonished eyes rested on a nicely dressed boy (the hat alone excepted) who looked indeed like Dick, but so transformed in dress that it was difficult to be sure of his identity.

"What luck, Johnny?" repeated Dick.

Johnny surveyed him from head to foot in great bewilderment.

"Who be you?" he said.

"Well, that's a good one," laughed Dick; "so you don't know Dick?"

"Where'd you get all them clothes?" asked Johnny. "Have you been stealin'?"

"Say that again, and I'll lick you. No, I've lent my clothes to a young feller as was goin' to a party, and didn't have none fit to wear, and so I put on my second-best for a change."

Without deigning any further explanation, Dick went off, followed by the astonished gaze of Johnny Nolan, who could not quite make up his mind whether the neat-looking boy he had been talking with was really Ragged Dick or not.

In order to reach Chatham Street it was necessary to cross Broadway. This was easier proposed than done. There is always such a throng of omnibuses, drays, carriages, and vehicles of all kinds in the neighborhood of the Astor House, that the crossing is formidable to one who is not used to it. Dick made nothing of it, dodging in and out among the horses and wagons with perfect self-possession. Reaching the opposite sidewalk, he looked back, and found that Frank had retreated in dismay, and that the width of the street was between them.

"Come across!" called out Dick.

"I don't see any chance," said Frank, looking anxiously at the prospect before him. "I'm afraid of being run over."

"If you are, you can sue 'em for damages," said Dick.

Finally Frank got safely over after several narrow escapes, as he considered them.

"Is it always so crowded?" he asked.

"A good deal worse sometimes," said Dick. "I knowed a young man once who waited six hours for a chance to cross, and at last got run over by an omnibus, leaving a widder and a large family of orphan children. His widder, a beautiful young woman, was obliged to start a peanut and apple stand. There she is now."

"Where?"

Dick pointed to a hideous old woman, of large proportions, wearing a bonnet of immense size, who presided over an apple-stand close by.

Frank laughed.

"If that is the case," he said, "I think I will patronize her."

"Leave it to me," said Dick, winking.

He advanced gravely to the apple-stand, and said, "Old lady, have you paid your taxes?"

The astonished woman opened her eyes.

"I'm a gov'ment officer," said Dick, "sent by the mayor to collect your taxes. I'll take it in apples just to oblige. That big red one will about pay what you're owin' to the gov'ment."

"I don't know nothing about no taxes," said the old woman, in bewilderment.

"Then," said Dick, "I'll let you off this time. Give us two of your best apples, and my friend here, the President of the Common Council, will pay you."

Frank, smiling, paid three cents apiece for the apples, and they sauntered on, Dick remarking, "If these apples ain't good, old lady, we'll return 'em, and get our money back." This would have been rather difficult in his case, as the apple was already half consumed.

Chatham Street, where they wished to go, being on the East side, the two boys crossed the Park. This is an enclosure of about ten acres, which years ago was covered with a green sward, but is now a great thoroughfare for pedestrians and contains several important public buildings. Dick pointed out the City Hall, the Hall of Records, and the Rotunda. The former is a white building of large size, and surmounted by a cupola.

"That's where the mayor's office is," said Dick. "Him and me are very good friends. I once blacked his boots by partic'lar appointment. That's the way I pay my city taxes."

CHAPTER V

Chatham Street and Broadway

THEY were soon in Chatham Street, walking between rows of ready-made clothing shops, many of which had half their stock in trade exposed on the sidewalk. The proprietors of these establishments stood at the doors, watching attentively the passersby, extending urgent invitations to any who even glanced at the goods to enter.

"Walk in, young gentlemen," said a stout man, at the entrance of one shop.

"No, I thank you," replied Dick, "as the fly said to the spider."

"We're selling off at less than cost."

"Of course you be. That's where you makes your money," said Dick. "There ain't nobody of any enterprise that pretends to make any profit on his goods."

The Chatham Street trader looked after our hero as if he didn't quite comprehend him; but Dick, without waiting for a reply, passed on with his companion.

In some of the shops auctions seemed to be going on.

"I am only offered two dollars, gentlemen, for this elegant pair of doeskin pants, made of the very best of cloth. It's a frightful sacrifice. Who'll give an eighth? Thank you, sir. Only seventeen shillings! Why the cloth cost more by the yard!"

This speaker was standing on a little platform haranguing to three men, holding in his hand meanwhile a pair of pants very loose in the legs, and presenting a cheap Bowery look.

Frank and Dick paused before the shop door, and finally saw them knocked down to rather a verdant-looking individual at three dollars.

"Clothes seem to be pretty cheap here," said Frank.

"Yes, but Baxter Street is the cheapest place."

"Is it?"

"Yes. Johnny Nolan got a whole rig-out there last week, for a dollar—coat, cap, vest, pants, and shoes. They was very good measure, too, like my best clothes that I took off to oblige you."

"I shall know where to come for clothes next time," said Frank, laughing. "I had no idea the city was so much cheaper than the country. I suppose the Baxter Street tailors are fashionable?"

"In course they are. Me and Horace Greeley always go there for clothes. When Horace gets a new suit, I always have one made just like it; but I can't go the white hat. It ain't becomin' to my style of beauty."

A little farther on a man was standing out on the sidewalk, distributing small printed handbills. One was handed to Frank, which he read as follows—

"GRAND CLOSING-OUT SALE!—A variety of Beautiful and Costly Articles for Sale, at a Dollar apiece. Unparalleled Inducements! Walk in, Gentlemen!"

"Whereabouts is this sale?" asked Frank.

"In here, young gentlemen," said a black-whiskered individual, who appeared suddenly on the scene. "Walk in."

"Shall we go in, Dick?"

"It's a swindlin' shop," said Dick, in a low voice. "I've been there. That man's a reg'lar cheat. He's seen me before, but he don't know me coz of my clothes."

"Step in and see the articles," said the man, persuasively. "You needn't buy, you know."

"Are all the articles worth more'n a dollar?" asked Dick.

"Yes," said the other, "and some worth a great deal more."

"Such as what?"

"Well, there's a silver pitcher worth twenty dollars."

"And you sell it for a dollar. That's very kind of you," said Dick, innocently.

"Walk in, and you'll understand it."

"No, I guess not," said Dick. "My servants is so dishonest that I wouldn't like to trust 'em with a silver pitcher. Come along, Frank. I hope you'll succeed in your charitable enterprise of supplyin' the public with silver pitchers at nineteen dollars less than they are worth."

"How does he manage, Dick?" asked Frank, as they went on.

"All his articles are numbered, and he makes you pay a dollar, and then shakes some dice, and whatever the figgers come to, is the number of the article you draw. Most of 'em ain't worth sixpence."

A hat and cap store being close at hand, Dick and Frank went in. For seventy-five cents, which Frank insisted on paying, Dick succeeded in getting quite a neat-looking cap, which corresponded much better with his appearance than the one he had on. The last, not being considered worth keeping, Dick dropped on the sidewalk, from which, on looking back, he saw it picked up by a brother boot-black who appeared to consider it better than his own.

They retraced their steps and went up Chambers Street to Broadway. At the corner of Broadway and Chambers Street is a large white marble warehouse, which attracted Frank's attention.

"What building is that?" he asked, with interest.

"That belongs to my friend. A. T. Stewart," said Dick. "It's the biggest store on Broadway.* If I ever retire from boot-blackin', and go into mercantile pursuits, I may buy him out, or build another store that'll take the shine off this one."

"Were you ever in the store?" asked Frank.

"No," said Dick; "but I'm intimate with one of Stewart's partners. He is a cash boy, and does nothing but take money all day."

"A very agreeable employment," said Frank, laughing.

"Yes," said Dick, "I'd like to be in it."

The boys crossed to the West side of Broadway, and walked slowly up the street. To Frank it was a very interesting spectacle. Accustomed to the quiet of the country, there was something fascinating in the crowds of people thronging the sidewalks, and the great variety of vehicles constantly passing and repassing in the street. Then again the shop-windows with their multifarious contents interested and amused him, and he was constantly checking Dick to look in at some well-stocked window.

"I don't see how so many shopkeepers can find people enough to buy of them," he said. "We haven't got but two stores in our village, and Broadway seems to be full of them."

"Yes," said Dick; "and it's pretty much the same in the avenoos, 'specially the Third, Sixth, and Eighth avenoos. The Bowery, too, is a great place for shoppin'. There everybody sells cheaper'n anybody else, and nobody pretends to make no profit on their goods."

"Where's Barnum's Museum?" asked Frank.

"Oh, that's down nearly opposite the Astor House," said Dick. "Didn't you see a great building with lots of flags?"

"Yes."

---

* Mr. Stewart's Tenth Street store was not open at the time Dick spoke.

"Well, that's Barnum's.* That's where the Happy Family live, and the lions, and bears, and curiosities generally. It's a tip-top place. Haven't you ever been there? It's most as good as the Old Bowery, only the plays isn't quite so excitin'."

"I'll go if I get time," said Frank. "There is a boy at home who came to New York a month ago, and went to Barnum's, and has been talking about it ever since, so I suppose it must be worth seeing."

"They've got a great play at the Old Bowery now," pursued Dick. "'Tis called the 'Demon of the Danube.' The Demon falls in love with a young woman, and drags her by the hair up to the top of a steep rock where his castle stands."

"That's a queer way of showing his love," said Frank, laughing.

"She didn't want to go with him, you know, but was in love with another chap. When he heard about his girl bein' carried off, he felt awful, and swore an oath not to rest till he had got her free. Well, at last he got into the castle by some underground passage, and he and the Demon had a fight. Oh, it was bully seein' 'em roll round on the stage, cuttin' and slashin' at each other."

"And which got the best of it?"

"At first the Demon seemed to be ahead, but at last the young Baron got him down, and struck a dagger into his heart, sayin', 'Die, false and perjured villain! The dogs shall feast upon thy carcass!' and then the Demon give an awful howl and died. Then the Baron seized his body, and threw it over the precipice."

"It seems to me the actor who plays the Demon ought to get extra pay, if he has to be treated that way."

"That's so," said Dick; "but I guess he's used to it. It seems to agree with his constitution."

* Since destroyed by fire, and rebuilt farther up Broadway, and again burned down in February.

"What building is that?" asked Frank, pointing to a structure several rods back from the street, with a large yard in front. It was an unusual sight for Broadway, all the other buildings in that neighborhood being even with the street.

"That is the New York Hospital," said Dick. "They're a rich institution, and take care of sick people on very reasonable terms."

"Did you ever go in there?"

"Yes," said Dick; "there was a friend of mine, Johnny Mullen, he was a newsboy, got run over by a omnibus as he was crossin' Broadway down near Park Place. He was carried to the Hospital, and me and some of his friends paid his board while he was there. It was only three dollars a week, which was very cheap, considerin' all the care they took of him. I got leave to come and see him while he was here. Everything looked so nice and comfortable, that I thought a little of coaxin' a omnibus driver to run over me, so I might go there too."

"Did your friend have to have his leg cut off?" asked Frank, interested.

"No," said Dick; "though there was a young student there that was very anxious to have it cut off; but it wasn't done, and Johnny is around the streets as well as ever."

While this conversation was going on they reached No. 365, at the corner of Franklin Street.*

"That's Taylor's Saloon," said Dick. "When I come into a fortun' I shall take my meals there reg'lar."

"I have heard of it very often," said Frank. "It is said to be very elegant. Suppose we go in and take an ice-cream. It will give us a chance to see it to better advantage."

"Thank you," said Dick; "I think that's the most agreeable way of seein' the place myself."

The boys entered, and found themselves in a spacious

---

* Now the office of the Merchants' Union Express Company.

and elegant saloon, resplendent with gilding, and adorned on all sides by costly mirrors. They sat down to a small table with a marble top, and Frank gave the order.

"It reminds me of Aladdin's palace," said Frank, looking about him.

"Does it?" said Dick; "he must have had plenty of money."

"He had an old lamp, which he had only to rub, when the Slave of the Lamp would appear, and do whatever he wanted."

"That must have been a valooable lamp. I'd be willin' to give all my Erie shares for it."

There was a tall, gaunt individual at the next table, who apparently heard this last remark of Dick's. Turning towards our hero, he said, "May I inquire, young man, whether you are largely interested in this Erie Railroad?"

"I haven't got no property except what's invested in Erie," said Dick, with a comical side-glance at Frank.

"Indeed! I suppose the investment was made by your guardian."

"No," said Dick; "I manage my property myself."

"And I presume your dividends have not been large?"

"Why, no," said Dick; "you're about right there. They haven't."

"As I supposed. It's poor stock. Now, my young friend, I can recommend a much better investment, which will yield you a large annual income. I am agent of the Excelsior Copper Mining Company, which possesses one of the most productive mines in the world. It's sure to yield fifty per cent, on the investment. Now, all you have to do is to sell out your Erie shares, and invest in our stock, and I'll insure you a fortune in three years. How many shares did you say you had?"

"I didn't say, that I remember," said Dick. "Your offer is very kind and obligin', and as soon as I get time I'll see about it."

"I hope you will," said the stranger. "Permit me to give

you my card. 'Samuel Snap, No.— Wall Street.' I shall be most happy to receive a call from you, and exhibit the maps of our mine. I should be glad to have you mention the matter also to your friends. I am confident you could do no greater service than to induce them to embark in our enterprise."

"Very good," said Dick.

Here the stranger left the table, and walked up to the desk to settle his bill.

"You see what it is to be a man of fortun', Frank," said Dick, "and wear good clothes. I wonder what that chap'll say when he sees me blackin' boots to-morrow in the street?"

"Perhaps you earn your money more honorably than he does, after all," said Frank. "Some of these mining companies are nothing but swindles, got up to cheat people out of their money."

"He's welcome to all he gets out of me," said Dick.

CHAPTER VI

⟶

Up Broadway to Madison Square

As the boys pursued their way up Broadway, Dick pointed out the prominent hotels and places of amusement. Frank was particularly struck with the imposing fronts of the St. Nicholas and Metropolitan Hotels, the former of white marble, the latter of a subdued brown hue, but not less elegant in its internal appointments. He was not surprised to be informed that each of these splendid structures cost with the furnishing not far from a million dollars.

At Eighth Street Dick turned to the right, and pointed out the Clinton Hall Building now occupied by the Mercantile Library, comprising at that time over fifty thousand volumes.*

A little farther on they came to a large building standing by itself just at the opening of Third and Fourth Avenues, and with one side on each.

"What is that building?" asked Frank.

"That's the Cooper Institute," said Dick; "built by Mr.

---

* Now not far from one hundred thousand.

Cooper, a particular friend of mine. Me and Peter Cooper used to go to school together."

"What is there inside?" asked Frank.

"There's a hall for public meetin's and lectures in the basement, and a readin' room and a picture gallery up above," said Dick.

Directly opposite Cooper Institute, Frank saw a very large building of brick, covering about an acre of ground.

"Is that a hotel?" he asked.

"No," said Dick; "that's the Bible House. It's the place where they make Bibles. I was in there once,—saw a big pile of 'em."

"Did you ever read the Bible?" asked Frank, who had some idea of the neglected state of Dick's education.

"No," said Dick; "I've heard it's a good book, but I never read one. I ain't much on readin'. It makes my head ache."

"I suppose you can't read very fast."

"I can read the little words pretty well, but the big ones is what stick me."

"If I lived in the city, you might come every evening to me, and I would teach you."

"Would you take so much trouble about me?" asked Dick, earnestly.

"Certainly; I should like to see you getting on. There isn't much chance of that if you don't know how to read and write."

"You're a good feller," said Dick, gratefully. "I wish you did live in New York. I'd like to know somethin'. Whereabouts do you live?"

"About fifty miles off, in a town on the left bank of the Hudson. I wish you'd come up and see me sometime. I would like to have you come and stop two or three days."

"Honor bright?"

"I don't understand."

"Do you mean it?" asked Dick, incredulously.

"Of course I do. Why shouldn't I?"

"What would your folks say if they knowed you asked a boot-black to visit you?"

"You are none the worse for being a boot-black, Dick."

"I ain't used to genteel society," said Dick. "I shouldn't know how to behave."

"Then I could show you. You won't be a boot-black all your life, you know."

"No," said Dick; "I'm goin' to knock off when I get to be ninety."

"Before that, I hope," said Frank, smiling.

"I really wish I could get somethin' else to do," said Dick, soberly. "I'd like to be a office boy, and learn business, and grow up 'spectable."

"Why don't you try, and see if you can't get a place, Dick?"

"Who'd take Ragged Dick?"

"But you ain't ragged now, Dick."

"No," said Dick; "I look a little better than I did in my Washington coat and Louis Napoleon pants. But if I got in a office, they wouldn't give me more'n three dollars a week, and I couldn't live 'spectable on that."

"No, I suppose not," said Frank, thoughtfully. "But you would get more at the end of the first year."

"Yes," said Dick; "but by that time I'd be nothin' but skin and bones."

Frank laughed. "That reminds me," he said, "of the story of an Irishman, who, out of economy, thought he would teach his horse to feed on shavings. So he provided the horse with a pair of green spectacles which made the shavings look eatable. But unfortunately, just as the horse got learned, he up and died."

"The hoss must have been a fine specimen of architectur' by the time he got through," remarked Dick.

"Whereabouts are we now?" asked Frank, as they emerged from Fourth Avenue into Union Square.

"That is Union Park," said Dick, pointing to a beautiful enclosure, in the centre of which was a pond, with a fountain playing.

"Is that the statue of General Washington?" asked Frank, pointing to a bronze equestrian statue on a granite pedestal.

"Yes," said Dick; "he's growed some since he was President. If he'd been as tall as that when he fit in the Revolution, he'd have walloped the Britishers some, I reckon."

Frank looked up at the statue, which is fourteen and a half feet high, and acknowledged the justice of Dick's remark.

"How about the coat, Dick?" he asked. "Would it fit you?"

"Well, it might be rather loose," said Dick. "I ain't much more'n ten feet high with my boots off."

"No, I should think not," said Frank, smiling. "You're a queer boy, Dick."

"Well, I've been brought up queer. Some boys is born with a silver spoon in their mouth. Victoria's boys is born with a gold spoon, set with di'monds; but gold and silver was scarce when I was born, and mine was pewter."

"Perhaps the gold and silver will come by and by, Dick. Did you ever hear of Dick Whittington?"

"Never did. Was he a Ragged Dick?"

"I shouldn't wonder if he was. At any rate he was very poor when he was a boy, but he didn't stay so. Before he died, he became Lord Mayor of London."

"Did he?" asked Dick, looking interested. "How did he do it?"

"Why, you see, a rich merchant took pity on him, and gave him a home in his own house, where he used to stay with the servants, being employed in little errands. One day the merchant noticed Dick picking up pins and needles that had been dropped, and asked him why he did it. Dick told him he was going to sell them when he got enough. The merchant was pleased with his saving disposition, and when soon after, he was going to send a vessel to foreign parts, he told Dick he might send anything he pleased in it, and it should be sold to his advantage. Now Dick had nothing in the world but a kitten which had been given him a short time before."

"How much taxes did he have to pay on it?" asked Dick.

"Not very high, probably. But having only the kitten, he concluded to send it along. After sailing a good many months, during which the kitten grew up to be a strong cat, the ship touched at an island never before known, which happened to be infested with rats and mice to such an extent that they worried everybody's life out, and even ransacked the king's palace. To make a long story short, the captain, seeing how matters stood, brought Dick's cat ashore, and she soon made the rats and mice scatter. The king was highly delighted when he saw what havoc she made among the rats and mice, and resolved to have her at any price. So he offered a great quantity of gold for her, which, of course, the captain was glad to accept. It was faithfully carried back to Dick, and laid the foundation of his fortune. He prospered as he grew up, and in time became a very rich merchant, respected by all, and before he died was elected Lord Mayor of London."

"That's a pretty good story," said Dick; "but I don't believe all the cats in New York will ever make me mayor."

"No, probably not, but you may rise in some other way. A good many distinguished men have once been poor boys. There's hope for you, Dick, if you'll try."

"Nobody ever talked to me so before," said Dick. "They just called me Ragged Dick, and told me I'd grow up to be a vagabone (boys who are better educated need not be surprised at Dick's blunders) and come to the gallows."

"Telling you so won't make it turn out so, Dick. If you'll try to be somebody, and grow up into a respectable member of society, you will. You may not become rich—it isn't everybody that becomes rich, you know—but you can obtain a good position, and be respected."

"I'll try," said Dick, earnestly. "I needn't have been Ragged Dick so long if I hadn't spent my money in goin' to the theatre, and treatin' boys to oyster-stews, and bettin' money on cards, and such like."

"Have you lost money that way?"

"Lots of it. One time I saved up five dollars to buy me a new rig-out, cos my best suit was all in rags, when Limpy Jim wanted me to play a game with him."

"Limpy Jim?" said Frank, interrogatively.

"Yes, he's lame; that's what makes us call him Limpy Jim."

"I suppose you lost?"

"Yes, I lost every penny, and had to sleep out, cos I hadn't a cent to pay for lodgin'. 'Twas a awful cold night, and I got most froze."

"Wouldn't Jim let you have any of the money he had won to pay for a lodging?"

"No; I axed him for five cents, but he wouldn't let me have it."

"Can you get lodging for five cents?" asked Frank, in surprise.

"Yes," said Dick, "but not at the Fifth Avenue Hotel. That's it right out there."

CHAPTER VII

The Pocket–book

THEY had reached the junction of Broadway and of Fifth Avenue. Before them was a beautiful park of ten acres. On the left-hand side was a large marble building, presenting a fine appearance with its extensive white front. This was the building at which Dick pointed.

"Is that the Fifth Avenue Hotel?" asked Frank. "I've heard of it often. My uncle William always stops there when he comes to New York."

"I once slept on the outside of it," said Dick. "They was very reasonable in their charges, and told me I might come again."

"Perhaps sometime you'll be able to sleep inside," said Frank.

"I guess that'll be when Queen Victoria goes to the Five Points to live."

"It looks like a palace," said Frank. "The queen needn't be ashamed to live in such a beautiful building as that."

Though Frank did not know it, one of the queen's palaces is far from being as fine a looking building as the Fifth Ave-

nue Hotel. St. James' Palace is a very ugly-looking brick
structure, and appears much more like a factory than like the
home of royalty. There are few hotels in the world as fine-
looking as this democratic institution.

At that moment a gentleman passed them on the sidewalk, who looked back at Dick, as if his face seemed familiar.

"I know that man," said Dick, after he had passed. "He's
one of my customers."

"What is his name?"

"I don't know."

"He looked back as if he thought he knew you."

"He would have knowed me at once if it hadn't been for
my new clothes," said Dick. "I don't look much like Ragged
Dick now."

"I suppose your face looked familiar."

"All but the dirt," said Dick, laughing. "I don't always
have the chance of washing my face and hands in the Astor
House."

"You told me," said Frank, "that there was a place where
you could get lodging for five cents. Where's that?"

"It's the Newsboys' Lodgin' House, on Fulton Street,"
said Dick, "up over the 'Sun' office. It's a good place. I don't
know what us boys would do without it. They give you supper for six cents, and a bed for five cents more."

"I suppose some boys don't even have the five cents to
pay,—do they?"

"They'll trust the boys," said Dick. "But I don't like to
get trusted. I'd be ashamed to get trusted for five cents, or
ten either. One night I was comin' down Chatham Street,
with fifty cents in my pocket. I was goin' to get a good
oyster-stew, and then go to the lodgin' house; but somehow
it slipped through a hole in my trowses-pocket, and I hadn't
a cent left. If it had been summer I shouldn't have cared, but
it's rather tough stayin' out winter nights."

Frank, who had always possessed a good home of his own, found it hard to realize that the boy who was walking at his side had actually walked the streets in the cold without a home, or money to procure the common comfort of a bed.

"What did you do?" he asked, his voice full of sympathy.

"I went to the 'Times' office. I knowed one of the press-men, and he let me set down in a corner, where I was warm, and I soon got fast asleep."

"Why don't you get a room somewhere, and so always have a home to go to?"

"I dunno," said Dick. "I never thought of it. P'rhaps I may hire a furnished house on Madison Square."

"That's where Flora McFlimsey lived."

"I don't know her," said Dick, who had never read the popular poem of which she is the heroine.

While this conversation was going on, they had turned into Twenty-fifth Street, and had by this time reached Third Avenue.

Just before entering it, their attention was drawn to the rather singular conduct of an individual in front of them. Stopping suddenly, he appeared to pick up something from the sidewalk, and then looked about him in rather a confused way.

"I know his game," whispered Dick. "Come along and you'll see what it is."

He hurried Frank forward until they overtook the man, who had come to a stand-still.

"Have you found anything?" asked Dick.

"Yes," said the man, "I've found this."

He exhibited a wallet which seemed stuffed with bills, to judge from its plethoric appearance.

"Whew!" exclaimed Dick; "you're in luck."

"I suppose somebody has lost it," said the man, "and will offer a handsome reward."

"Which you'll get."

"Unfortunately I am obliged to take the next train to Boston. That's where I live. I haven't time to hunt up the owner."

"Then I suppose you'll take the pocket-book with you," said Dick, with assumed simplicity.

"I should like to leave it with some honest fellow who would see it returned to the owner," said the man, glancing at the boys.

"I'm honest," said Dick.

"I've no doubt of it," said the other. "Well, young man, I'll make you an offer. You take the pocket-book—"

"All right. Hand it over, then."

"Wait a minute. There must be a large sum inside. I shouldn't wonder if there might be a thousand dollars. The owner will probably give you a hundred dollars reward."

"Why don't you stay and get it?" asked Frank.

"I would, only there is sickness in my family, and I must get home as soon as possible. Just give me twenty dollars, and I'll hand you the pocket-book, and let you make whatever you can out of it. Come, that's a good offer. What do you say?"

Dick was well dressed, so that the other did not regard it as at all improbable that he might possess that sum. He was prepared, however, to let him have it for less, if necessary.

"Twenty dollars is a good deal of money," said Dick, appearing to hesitate.

"You'll get it back, and a good deal more," said the stranger, persuasively.

"I don't know but I shall. What would you do, Frank?"

"I don't know but I would," said Frank, "if you've got the money." He was not a little surprised to think that Dick had so much by him.

"I don't know but I will," said Dick, after some irresolution. "I guess I won't lose much."

"You can't lose anything," said the stranger briskly.

"Only be quick, for I must be on my way to the cars. I am afraid I shall miss them now."

Dick pulled out a bill from his pocket, and handed it to the stranger, receiving the pocket-book in return. At that moment a policeman turned the corner, and the stranger, hurriedly thrusting the bill into his pocket, without looking at it, made off with rapid steps.

"What is there in the pocket-book, Dick?" asked Frank in some excitement. "I hope there's enough to pay you for the money you gave him."

Dick laughed.

"I'll risk that," said he.

"But you gave him twenty dollars. That's a good deal of money."

"If I had given him as much as that, I should deserve to be cheated out of it."

"But you did,—didn't you?"

"He thought so."

"What was it, then?"

"It was nothing but a dry-goods circular got up to imitate a bank-bill."

Frank looked sober.

"You ought not to have cheated him, Dick," he said, reproachfully.

"Didn't he want to cheat me?"

"I don't know."

"What do you s'pose there is in that pocket-book?" asked Dick, holding it up.

Frank surveyed its ample proportions, and answered sincerely enough, "Money, and a good deal of it."

"There ain't stamps enough in it to buy a oyster-stew," said Dick. "If you don't believe it, just look while I open it."

So saying he opened the pocket-book, and showed Frank that it was stuffed out with pieces of blank paper, carefully folded up in the shape of bills. Frank, who was unused to city life, and had never heard anything of the "drop-game" looked amazed at this unexpected development.

"I knowed how it was all the time," said Dick. "I guess I got the best of him there. This wallet's worth somethin'. I shall use it to keep my stiffkit of Erie stock in, and all my other papers what ain't of no use to anybody but the owner."

"That's the kind of papers it's got in it now," said Frank, smiling.

"That's so!" said Dick.

"By hokey!" he exclaimed suddenly, "if there ain't the old chap comin' back ag'in. He looks as if he'd heard bad news from his sick family."

By this time the pocket-book dropper had come up.

Approaching the boys, he said in an undertone to Dick, "Give me back that pocket-book, you young rascal!"

"Beg your pardon, mister," said Dick, "but was you addressin' me?"

"Yes, I was."

"'Cause you called me by the wrong name. I've knowed some rascals, but I ain't the honor to belong to the family."

He looked significantly at the other as he spoke, which didn't improve the man's temper. Accustomed to swindle others, he did not fancy being practised upon in return.

"Give me back that pocket-book," he repeated in a threatening voice.

"Couldn't do it," said Dick, coolly. "I'm go'n' to restore it to the owner. The contents is so valooable that most likely the loss has made him sick, and he'll be likely to come down liberal to the honest finder."

"You gave me a bogus bill," said the man.

"It's what I use myself," said Dick.

"You've swindled me."

"I thought it was the other way."

"None of your nonsense," said the man angrily. "If you don't give up that pocket-book, I'll call a policeman."

"I wish you would," said Dick. "They'll know most likely whether it's Stewart or Astor that's lost the pocket-book, and I can get 'em to return it."

The "dropper," whose object it was to recover the pocket-book, in order to try the same game on a more satisfactory customer, was irritated by Dick's refusal, and above all by the coolness he displayed. He resolved to make one more attempt.

"Do you want to pass the night in the Tombs?" he asked.

"Thank you for your very obligin' proposal," said Dick; "but it ain't convenient to-day. Any other time, when you'd like to have me come and stop with you, I'm agreeable; but my two youngest children is down with the measles, and I expect I'll have to set up all night to take care of 'em. Is the Tombs, in gineral, a pleasant place of residence?"

Dick asked this question with an air of so much earnestness that Frank could scarcely forbear laughing, though it is hardly necessary to say that the dropper was by no means so inclined.

"You'll know sometime," he said, scowling.

"I'll make you a fair offer," said Dick. "If I get more'n fifty dollars as a reward for my honesty, I'll divide with you. But I say, ain't it most time to go back to your sick family in Boston?"

Finding that nothing was to be made out of Dick, the man strode away with a muttered curse.

"You were too smart for him, Dick," said Frank.

"Yes," said Dick, "I ain't knocked round the city streets all my life for nothin'."

CHAPTER VIII

Dick's Early History

"Have you always lived in New York, Dick?" asked Frank, after a pause.

"Ever since I can remember."

"I wish you'd tell me a little about yourself. Have you got any father or mother?"

"I ain't got no mother. She died when I wasn't but three years old. My father went to sea; but he went off before mother died, and nothin' was ever heard of him. I expect he got wrecked, or died at sea."

"And what became of you when your mother died?"

"The folks she boarded with took care of me, but they was poor, and they couldn't do much. When I was seven the woman died, and her husband went out West, and then I had to scratch for myself."

"At seven years old!" exclaimed Frank, in amazement.

"Yes," said Dick, "I was a little feller to take care of myself, but," he continued with pardonable pride, "I did it."

"What could you do?"

"Sometimes one thing, and sometimes another," said

Dick. "I changed my business accordin' as I had to. Sometimes I was a newsboy, and diffused intelligence among the
masses, as I heard somebody say once in a big speech he
made in the Park. Them was the times when Horace Greeley
and James Gordon Bennett made money."

"Through your enterprise?" suggested Frank.

"Yes," said Dick; "but I give it up after a while."

"What for?"

"Well, they didn't always put news enough in their papers, and people wouldn't buy 'em as fast as I wanted 'em
to. So one mornin' I was stuck on a lot of *Heralds,* and I
thought I'd make a sensation. So I called out 'GREAT NEWS!
QUEEN VICTORIA ASSASSINATED!' All my *Heralds* went off
like hot cakes, and I went off, too, but one of the gentlemen
what got sold remembered me, and said he'd have me took
up, and that's what made me change my business."

"That wasn't right, Dick," said Frank.

"I know it," said Dick; "but lots of boys does it."

"That don't make it any better."

"No," said Dick, "I was sort of ashamed at the time, 'specially about one poor old gentleman,—a Englishman he was.
He couldn't help cryin' to think the queen was dead, and his
hands shook when he handed me the money for the paper."

"What did you do next?"

"I went into the match business," said Dick; "but it was
small sales and small profits. Most of the people I called on
had just laid in a stock, and didn't want to buy. So one cold
night, when I hadn't money enough to pay for a lodgin', I
burned the last of my matches to keep me from freezin'. But it
cost too much to get warm that way, and I couldn't keep it up."

"You've seen hard times, Dick," said Frank, compassionately.

"Yes," said Dick, "I've knowed what it was to be hungry
and cold, with nothin' to eat or to warm me; but there's one
thing I never could do," he added proudly.

"What's that?"

"I never stole," said Dick. "It's mean and I wouldn't do it."

"Were you ever tempted to?"

"Lots of times. Once I had been goin' round all day, and hadn't sold any matches, except three cents' worth early in the mornin'. With that I bought an apple, thinkin' I should get some more bimeby. When evenin' come I was awful hungry. I went into a baker's just to look at the bread. It made me feel kind o' good just to look at the bread and cakes, and I thought maybe they would give me some. I asked 'em wouldn't they give me a loaf, and take their pay in matches. But they said they'd got enough matches to last three months; so there wasn't any chance for a trade. While I was standin' at the stove warmin' me, the baker went into a back room, and I felt so hungry I thought I would take just one loaf, and go off with it. There was such a big pile I don't think he'd have known it."

"But you didn't do it?"

"No, I didn't, and I was glad of it, for when the man came in ag'in, he said he wanted some one to carry some cake to a lady in St. Mark's Place. His boy was sick, and he hadn't no one to send; so he told me he'd give me ten cents if I would go. My business wasn't very pressin' just then, so I went, and when I come back, I took my pay in bread and cakes. Didn't they taste good, though?"

"So you didn't stay long in the match business, Dick?"

"No, I couldn't sell enough to make it pay. Then there was some folks that wanted me to sell cheaper to them; so I couldn't make any profit. There was one old lady—she was rich, too, for she lived in a big brick house—beat me down so, that I didn't make no profit at all; but she wouldn't buy without, and I hadn't sold none that day; so I let her have them. I don't see why rich folks should be so hard upon a poor boy that wants to make a livin'."

"There's a good deal of meanness in the world, I'm afraid, Dick."

"If everybody was like you and your uncle," said Dick, "there would be some chance for poor people. If I was rich I'd try to help 'em along."

"Perhaps you will be rich sometime, Dick."

Dick shook his head.

"I'm afraid all my wallets will be like this," said Dick, indicating the one he had received from the dropper, "and will be full of papers what ain't of no use to anybody except the owner."

"That depends very much on yourself, Dick," said Frank. "Stewart wasn't always rich, you know."

"Wasn't he?"

"When he first came to New York as a young man he was a teacher, and teachers are not generally very rich. At last he went into business, starting in a small way, and worked his way up by degrees. But there was one thing he determined in the beginning; that he would be strictly honorable in all his dealings, and never overreach any one for the sake of making money. If there was a chance for him, Dick, there is a chance for you."

"He knowed enough to be a teacher, and I'm awful ignorant," said Dick.

"But you needn't stay so."

"How can I help it?"

"Can't you learn at school?"

"I can't go to school 'cause I've got my livin' to earn. It wouldn't do me much good if I learned to read and write, and just as I'd got learned I starved to death."

"But are there no night-schools?"

"Yes."

"Why don't you go? I suppose you don't work in the evenings."

"I never cared much about it," said Dick, "and that's the truth. But since I've got to talkin' with you, I think more about it. I guess I'll begin to go."

"I wish you would, Dick. You'll make a smart man if you only get a little education."

"Do you think so?" asked Dick, doubtfully.

"I know so. A boy who has earned his own living ever since he was seven years old must have something in him. I feel very much interested in you, Dick. You've had a hard time of it so far in life, but I think better times are in store. I want you to do well, and I feel sure you can if you only try."

"You're a good fellow," said Dick, gratefully. "I'm afraid I'm a pretty rough customer, but I ain't as bad as some. I mean to turn over a new leaf, and try to grow up 'spectable."

"There've been a great many boys begin as low down as you, Dick, that have grown up respectable and honored. But they had to work pretty hard for it."

"I'm willin' to work hard," said Dick.

"And you must not only work hard, but work in the right way."

"What's the right way?"

"You began in the right way when you determined never to steal, or do anything mean or dishonorable, however strongly tempted to do so. That will make people have confidence in you when they come to know you. But, in order to succeed well, you must manage to get as good an education as you can. Until you do, you cannot get a position in an office or counting-room, even to run errands."

"That's so," said Dick, soberly. "I never thought how awful ignorant I was till now."

"That can be remedied with perseverance," said Frank. "A year will do a great deal for you."

"I'll go to work and see what I can do," said Dick, energetically.

CHAPTER IX

A Scene in a Third Avenue Car

THE boys had turned into Third Avenue, a long street, which, commencing just below the Cooper Institute, runs out to Harlem. A man came out of a side street, uttering at intervals a monotonous cry which sounded like "glass puddin'."

"Glass pudding!" repeated Frank, looking in surprised wonder at Dick. "What does he mean?"

"Perhaps you'd like some," said Dick.

"I never heard of it before."

"Suppose you ask him what he charges for his puddin'."

Frank looked more narrowly at the man, and soon concluded that he was a glazier.

"Oh, I understand," he said. "He means 'glass put in.'"

Frank's mistake was not a singular one. The monotonous cry of these men certainly sounds more like "glass puddin'," than the words they intend to utter.

"Now," said Dick, "where shall we go?"

"I should like to see Central Park," said Frank. "Is it far off?"

"It is about a mile and a half from here," said Dick. "This

is Twenty-ninth Street, and the Park begins at Fifty-ninth Street."

It may be explained, for the benefit of readers who have never visited New York, that about a mile from the City Hall the cross-streets begin to be numbered in regular order. There is a continuous line of houses as far as One Hundred and Thirtieth Street, where may be found the terminus of the Harlem line of horse-cars. When the entire island is laid out and settled, probably the numbers will reach two hundred or more. Central Park, which lies between Fifty-ninth Street on the south, and One Hundred and Tenth Street on the north, is true to its name, occupying about the centre of the island. The distance between two parallel streets is called a block, and twenty blocks make a mile. It will therefore be seen that Dick was exactly right, when he said they were a mile and a half from Central Park.

"That is too far to walk," said Frank.

"'Twon't cost but six cents to ride," said Dick.

"You mean in the horse-cars?"

"Yes."

"All right then. We'll jump aboard the next car."

The Third Avenue and Harlem line of horse-cars is better patronized than any other in New York, thought not much can be said for the cars, which are usually dirty and over-crowded. Still, when it is considered that only seven cents are charged for the entire distance to Harlem, about seven miles from the City Hall, the fare can hardly be complained of. But of course most of the profit is made from the way-passengers who only ride a short distance.

A car was at that moment approaching, but it seemed pretty crowded.

"Shall we take that, or wait for another?" asked Frank.

"The next'll most likely be as bad," said Dick.

The boys accordingly signalled to the conductor to stop, and got on the front platform. They were obliged to stand up till the car reached Fortieth Street, when so many of the passengers had got off that they obtained seats.

Frank sat down beside a middle-aged woman, or lady, as she probably called herself, whose sharp visage and thin lips did not seem to promise a very pleasant disposition. When the two gentlemen who sat beside her arose, she spread her skirts in the endeavor to fill two seats. Disregarding this, the boys sat down.

"There ain't room for two," she said looking sourly at Frank.

"There were two here before."

"Well, there ought not to have been. Some people like to crowd in where they're not wanted."

"And some like to take up a double allowance of room," thought Frank; but he did not say so. He saw that the woman had a bad temper, and thought it wisest to say nothing.

Frank had never ridden up the city as far as this, and it was with much interest that he looked out of the car windows at the stores on either side. Third Avenue is a broad street, but in the character of its houses and stores it is quite inferior to Broadway, though better than some of the avenues further east. Fifth Avenue, as most of my readers already know, is the finest street in the city, being lined with splendid private residences, occupied by the wealthier classes. Many of the cross-streets also boast houses which may be considered palaces, so elegant are they externally and internally. Frank caught glimpses of some of these as he was carried towards the Park.

After the first conversation, already mentioned, with the lady at his side, he supposed he should have nothing further to do with her. But in this he was mistaken. While he was busy looking out of the car window, she plunged her hand into her pocket in search of her purse, which she was unable to find. Instantly she jumped to the conclusion that it had been stolen, and her suspicions fastened upon Frank, with whom she was already provoked for "crowding her," as she termed it.

"Conductor!" she exclaimed in a sharp voice.

"What's wanted, ma'am?" returned that functionary.

"I want you to come here right off."

"What's the matter?"

"My purse has been stolen. There was four dollars and eighty cents in it. I know, because I counted it when I paid my fare."

"Who stole it?"

"That boy," she said pointing to Frank, who listened to the charge in the most intense astonishment. "He crowded in here on purpose to rob me, and I want you to search him right off."

"That's a lie!" exclaimed Dick, indignantly.

"Oh, you're in league with him, I dare say," said the woman spitefully. "You're as bad as he is, I'll be bound."

"You're a nice female, you be!" said Dick, ironically.

"Don't you dare to call me a female, sir," said the lady, furiously.

"Why, you ain't a man in disguise, be you?" said Dick.

"You are very much mistaken, madam," said Frank, quietly. "The conductor may search me, if you desire it."

A charge of theft, made in a crowded car, of course made quite a sensation. Cautious passengers instinctively put their hands on their pockets, to make sure that they, too, had not been robbed. As for Frank, his face flushed, and he felt very indignant that he should even be suspected of so mean a crime. He had been carefully brought up, and been taught to regard stealing as low and wicked.

Dick, on the contrary, thought it a capital joke that such a charge should have been made against his companion. Though he had brought himself up, and known plenty of boys and men, too, who would steal, he had never done so himself. He thought it mean. But he could not be expected to regard it as Frank did. He had been too familiar with it in others to look upon it with horror.

Meanwhile the passengers rather sided with the boys. Appearances go a great ways, and Frank did not look like a thief.

"I think you must be mistaken, madam," said a gentleman sitting opposite. "The lad does not look as if he would steal."

"You can't tell by looks," said the lady, sourly. "They're deceitful; villains are generally well dressed."

"Be they?" said Dick. "You'd ought to see me with my Washington coat on. You'd think I was the biggest villain ever you saw."

"I've no doubt you are," said the lady, scowling in the direction of our hero.

"Thank you, ma'am," said Dick. " 'Tisn't often I get such fine compliments."

"None of your impudence," said the lady, wrathfully. "I believe you're the worst of the two."

Meanwhile the car had been stopped.

"How long are we going to stop here?" demanded a passenger, impatiently. "I'm in a hurry, if none of the rest of you are."

"I want my pocket-book," said the lady, defiantly.

"Well, ma'am, I haven't got it, and I don't see as it's doing you any good detaining us all here."

"Conductor, will you call a policeman to search that young scamp?" continued the aggrieved lady. "You don't expect I'm going to lose my money, and do nothing about it."

"I'll turn my pockets inside out if you want me to," said Frank, proudly. "There's no need of a policeman. The conductor, or any one else, may search me."

"Well, youngster," said the conductor, "if the lady agrees, I'll search you."

The lady signified her assent.

Frank accordingly turned his pockets inside out; but nothing was revealed except his own porte-monnaie and a penknife.

"Well, ma'am, are you satisfied?" asked the conductor.

"No, I ain't," said she, decidedly.

"You don't think he's got it still?"

"No, but he's passed it over to his confederate, that boy there that's so full of impudence."

"That's me," said Dick, comically.

"He confesses it," said the lady; "I want him searched."

"All right," said Dick, "I'm ready for the operation, only as I've got valooable property about me be careful not to drop any of my Erie Bonds."

The conductor's hand forthwith dove into Dick's pocket, and drew out a rusty jack-knife, a battered cent, about fifty cents in change, and the capacious pocket-book which he had received from the swindler who was anxious to get back to his sick family in Boston.

"Is that yours, ma'am?" asked the conductor, holding up the wallet which excited some amazement, by its size, among the other passengers.

"It seems to me you carry a large pocket-book for a young man of your age," said the conductor.

"That's what I carry my cash and valooable papers in," said Dick.

"I suppose that isn't yours, ma'am," said the conductor, turning to the lady.

"No," said she, scornfully. "I wouldn't carry round such a great wallet at that. Most likely he's stolen it from somebody else."

"What a prime detective you'd be!" said Dick. "P'rhaps you know who I took it from."

"I don't know but my money's in it," said the lady, sharply. "Conductor, will you open that wallet, and see what there is in it?"

"Don't disturb the valooable papers," said Dick, in a tone of pretended anxiety.

The contents of the wallet excited some amusement among the passengers.

"There don't seem to be much money here," said the conductor, taking out a roll of tissue paper cut out in the shape of bills, and rolled up.

"No," said Dick. "Didn't I tell you them were papers of no valoo to anybody but the owner? If the lady'd like to borrow, I won't charge no interest."

"Where is my money, then?" said the lady, in some discomfiture. "I shouldn't wonder if one of the young scamps had thrown it out of the window."

"You'd better search your pocket once more," said the gentleman opposite. "I don't believe either of the boys is in fault. They don't look to me as if they would steal."

"Thank you, sir," said Frank.

The lady followed out the suggestion, and, plunging her hand once more into her pocket, drew out a small portemonnaie. She hardly knew whether to be glad or sorry at this discovery. It placed her in rather an awkward position after the fuss she had made, and the detention to which she had subjected the passengers, now, as it proved, for nothing.

"Is that the pocket-book you thought stolen?" asked the conductor.

"Yes," said she, rather confusedly.

"Then you've been keeping me waiting all this time for nothing," he said, sharply. "I wish you'd take care to be sure next time before you make such a disturbance for nothing. I've lost five minutes, and shall not be on time."

"I can't help it," was the cross reply; "I didn't know it was in my pocket."

"It seems to me you owe an apology to the boys you accused of a theft which they have not committed," said the gentleman opposite.

"I shan't apologize to anybody," said the lady, whose temper was not of the best; "least of all to such whipper-snappers as they are."

"Thank you, ma'am," said Dick, comically, "your hand-some apology is accepted. It ain't of no consequence, only I didn't like to expose the contents of my valooable pocket-book, for fear it might excite the envy of some of my poor neighbors."

"You're a character," said the gentleman who had already spoken, with a smile.

"A bad character!" muttered the lady.

But it was quite evident that the sympathies of those pres-ent were against the lady, and on the side of the boys who had been falsely accused, while Dick's drollery had created considerable amusement.

The cars had now reached Fifty-ninth Street, the southern boundary of the Park, and here our hero and his companion got off.

"You'd better look out for pickpockets, my lad," said the conductor, pleasantly. "That big wallet of yours might prove a great temptation."

"That's so," said Dick. "That's the misfortin' of being rich. Astor and me don't sleep much for fear of burglars breakin' in and robbin' us of our valooable treasures. Some-times I think I'll give all my money to an Orphan Asylum, and take it out in board. I guess I'd make money by the oper-ation."

While Dick was speaking, the car rolled away, and the boys turned up Fifty-ninth Street, for two long blocks yet separated them from the Park.

CHAPTER X

Introduces a Victim
of Misplaced Confidence

"WHAT a queer chap you are, Dick!" said Frank laughing. "You always seem to be in good spirits."

"No, I ain't always. Sometimes I have the blues."

"When?"

"Well, once last winter it was awful cold, and there was big holes in my shoes, and my gloves and all my warm clothes was at the tailor's. I felt as if life was sort of tough, and I'd like it if some rich man would adopt me, and give me plenty to eat and drink and wear, without my havin' to look so sharp after it. Then agin' when I've seen boys with good homes, and fathers, and mothers, I've thought I'd like to have somebody to care for me."

Dick's tone changed as he said this, from his usual levity, and there was a touch of sadness in it. Frank, blessed with a good home and indulgent parents, could not help pitying the friendless boy who had found life such up-hill work.

"Don't say you have no one to care for you, Dick," he said, lightly laying his hand on Dick's shoulder. "I will care for you."

"Will you?"

"If you will let me."

"I wish you would," said Dick, earnestly. "I'd like to feel that I have one friend who cares for me."

Central Park was now before them, but it was far from presenting the appearance which it now exhibits. It had not been long since work had been commenced upon it, and it was still very rough and unfinished. A rough tract of land, two miles and a half from north to south, and a half a mile broad, very rocky in parts, was the material from which the Park Commissioners have made the present beautiful enclosure. There were no houses of good appearance near it, buildings being limited mainly to rude temporary huts used by the workmen who were employed in improving it. The time will undoubtedly come when the Park will be surrounded by elegant residences, and compare favorably in this respect with the most attractive parts of any city in the world. But at the time when Frank and Dick visited it, not much could be said in favor either of the Park or its neighborhood.

"If this is Central Park," said Frank, who naturally felt disappointed, "I don't think much of it. My father's got a large pasture that is much nicer."

"It'll look better some time," said Dick. "There ain't much to see now but rocks. We will take a walk over it if you want to."

"No," said Frank, "I've seen as much of it as I want to. Besides, I feel tired."

"Then we'll go back. We can take the Sixth Avenue cars. They will bring us out at Vesey Street, just beside the Astor House."

"All right," said Frank. "That will be the best course. I hope," he added, laughing, "our agreeable lady friend won't be there. I don't care about being accused of *stealing* again."

"She was a tough one," said Dick. "Wouldn't she make a

nice wife for a man that likes to live in hot water, and didn't mind bein' scalded two or three times a day?"

"Yes, I think she'd just suit him. Is that the right car, Dick?"

"Yes, jump in, and I'll follow."

The Sixth Avenue is lined with stores, many of them of very good appearance, and would make a very respectable principal street for a good-sized city. But it is only one of several long business streets which run up the island, and illustrate the extent and importance of the city to which they belong.

No incidents worth mentioning took place during their ride down town. In about three-quarters of an hour the boys got out of the car beside the Astor House.

"Are you goin' in now, Frank?" asked Dick.

"That depends upon whether you have anything else to show me."

"Wouldn't you like to go to Wall Street?"

"That's the street where there are so many bankers and brokers,—isn't it?"

"Yes, I s'pose you ain't afraid of bulls and bears,—are you?"

"Bulls and bears?" repeated Frank, puzzled.

"Yes."

"What are they?"

"The bulls is what tries to make the stocks go up, and the bears is what try to growl 'em down."

"Oh, I see. Yes, I'd like to go."

Accordingly they walked down on the west side of Broadway as far as Trinity Church, and then, crossing, entered a street not very wide or very long, but of very great importance. The reader would be astonished if he could know the amount of money involved in the transactions which take place in a single day in this street. It would be found that although Broadway is much greater in length, and lined with stores, it stands second to Wall Street in this respect.

"What is that large marble building?" asked Frank, pointing to a massive structure on the corner of Wall and Nassau Streets. It was in the form of a parallelogram, two hundred feet long by ninety wide, and about eighty feet in height, the ascent to the entrance being by eighteen granite steps.

"That's the Custom House," said Dick.

"It looks like pictures I've seen of the Parthenon at Athens," said Frank, meditatively.

"Where's Athens?" asked Dick. "It ain't in York State,—is it?"

"Not the Athens I mean, at any rate. It is in Greece, and was a famous city two thousand years ago."

"That's longer than I can remember," said Dick. "I can't remember distinctly more'n about a thousand years."

"What a chap you are, Dick! Do you know if we can go in?"

The boys ascertained, after a little inquiry, that they would be allowed to do so. They accordingly entered the Custom House and made their way up to the roof, from which they had a fine view of the harbor, the wharves crowded with shipping, and the neighboring shores of Long Island and New Jersey. Towards the north they looked down for many miles upon continuous lines of streets, and thousands of roofs, with here and there a church-spire rising above its neighbors. Dick had never before been up there, and he, as well as Frank, was interested in the grand view spread before them.

At length they descended, and were going down the granite steps on the outside of the building, when they were addressed by a young man, whose appearance is worth describing.

He was tall, and rather loosely put together, with small eyes and rather a prominent nose. His clothing had evidently not been furnished by a city tailor. He wore a blue coat with brass buttons, and pantaloons of rather scanty dimensions, which were several inches too short to cover his lower limbs.

He held in his hand a piece of paper, and his countenance wore a look of mingled bewilderment and anxiety.

"Be they a-payin' out money inside there?" he asked, indicating the interior by a motion of his hand.

"I guess so," said Dick. "Are you a-goin' in for some?"

"Wal, yes. I've got an order here for sixty dollars,—made a kind of speculation this morning."

"How was it?" asked Frank.

"Wal, you see I brought down some money to put in the bank, fifty dollars it was, and I hadn't justly made up my mind what bank to put it into, when a chap came up in a terrible hurry, and said it was very unfortunate, but the bank wasn't open, and he must have some money right off. He was obliged to go out of the city by the next train. I asked him how much he wanted. He said fifty dollars. I told him I'd got that, and he offered me a check on the bank for sixty, and I let him have it. I thought that was a pretty easy way to earn ten dollars, so I counted out the money and he went off. He told me I'd hear a bell ring when they began to pay out money. But I've waited most two hours, and I hain't heard it yet. I'd ought to be goin', for I told dad I'd be home to-night. Do you think I can get the money now?"

"Will you show me the check?" asked Frank, who had listened attentively to the countryman's story, and suspected that he had been made the victim of a swindler. It was made out upon the "Washington Bank," in the sum of sixty dollars, and was signed "Ephraim Smith."

"Washington Bank!" repeated Frank. "Dick, is there such a bank in the city?"

"Not as I knows on," said Dick. "Leastways I don't own any shares in it."

"Ain't this the Washington Bank?" asked the countryman, pointing to the building on the steps of which the three were now standing.

"No, it's the Custom House."

"And won't they give me any money for this?" asked the young man, the perspiration standing on his brow.

"I am afraid the man who gave it to you was a swindler," said Frank, gently.

"And won't I ever see my fifty dollars again?" asked the youth in agony.

"I am afraid not."

"What'll dad say?" ejaculated the miserable youth. "It makes me feel sick to think of it. I wish I had the feller here. I'd shake him out of his boots."

"What did he look like? I'll call a policeman and you shall describe him. Perhaps in that way you can get track of your money."

Dick called a policeman, who listened to the description, and recognized the operator as an experienced swindler. He assured the countryman that there was very little chance of his ever seeing his money again. The boys left the miserable youth loudly bewailing his bad luck, and proceeded on their way down the street.

"He's a baby," said Dick, contemptuously. "He'd ought to know how to take care of himself and his money. A feller has to look sharp in this city, or he'll lose his eye-teeth before he knows it."

"I suppose you never got swindled out of fifty dollars, Dick?"

"No, I don't carry no such small bills. I wish I did," he added.

"So do I, Dick. What's that building there at the end of the street?"

"That's the Wall-Street Ferry to Brooklyn."

"How long does it take to go across?"

"Not more'n five minutes."

"Suppose we just ride over and back."

"All right!" said Dick. "It's rather expensive; but if you don't mind, I don't."

"Why, how much does it cost?"

"Two cents apiece."

"I guess I can stand that. Let us go."

They passed the gate, paying the fare to a man who stood at the entrance, and were soon on the ferry-boat, bound for Brooklyn.

They had scarcely entered the boat, when Dick, grasping Frank by the arm, pointed to a man just outside of the gentlemen's cabin.

"Do you see that man, Frank?" he inquired.

"Yes, what of him?"

"He's the man that cheated the country chap out of his fifty dollars."

CHAPTER XI

Dick as a Detective

DICK'S ready identification of the rogue who had cheated the countryman surprised Frank.

"What makes you think it is he?" he asked.

"Because I've seen him before, and I know he's up to them kind of tricks. When I heard how he looked, I was sure I knowed him."

"Our recognizing him won't be of much use," said Frank. "It won't give back the countryman his money."

"I don't know," said Dick, thoughtfully. "Maybe I can get it."

"How?" asked Frank, incredulously.

"Wait a minute, and you'll see."

Dick left his companion, and went up to the man whom he suspected.

"Ephraim Smith," said Dick, in a low voice.

The man turned suddenly, and looked at Dick uneasily.

"What did you say?" he asked.

"I believe your name is Ephraim Smith," continued Dick.

"You're mistaken," said the man, and was about to move off.

"Stop a minute," said Dick. "Don't you keep your money in the Washington Bank?"

"I don't know any such bank. I'm in a hurry, young man, and I can't stop to answer any foolish questions."

The boat had by this time reached the Brooklyn pier, and Mr. Ephraim Smith seemed in a hurry to land.

"Look here," said Dick, significantly; "you'd better not go on shore unless you want to jump into the arms of a policeman."

"What do you mean?" asked the man, startled.

"That little affair of yours is known to the police," said Dick; "about how you got fifty dollars out of a greenhorn on a false check, and it mayn't be safe for you to go ashore."

"I don't know what you're talking about," said the swindler with affected boldness, though Dick could see that he was ill at ease.

"Yes, you do," said Dick. "There isn't but one thing to do. Just give me back that money, and I'll see that you're not touched. If you don't, I'll give you up to the first p'liceman we meet."

Dick looked so determined, and spoke so confidently, that the other, overcome by his fears, no longer hesitated, but passed a roll of bills to Dick and hastily left the boat.

All this Frank witnessed with great amazement, not understanding what influence Dick could have obtained over the swindler sufficient to compel restitution.

"How did you do it?" he asked eagerly.

"I told him I'd exert my influence with the president to have him tried by *habeas corpus*," said Dick.

"And of course that frightened him. But tell me, without joking, how you managed."

Dick gave a truthful account of what occurred, and then said, "Now we'll go back and carry the money."

"Suppose we don't find the poor countryman?"

"Then the p'lice will take care of it."

They remained on board the boat, and in five minutes were again in New York. Going up Wall Street, they met the countryman a little distance from the Custom House. His face was marked with the traces of deep anguish; but in his case even grief could not subdue the cravings of appetite. He had purchased some cakes of one of the old women who spread out for the benefit of passers-by an array of apples and seed-cakes, and was munching them with melancholy satisfaction.

"Hilloa!" said Dick. "Have you found your money?"

"No," ejaculated the young man, with a convulsive gasp. "I shan't ever see it again. The mean skunk's cheated me out of it. Consarn his picter! It took me most six months to save it up. I was workin' for Deacon Pinkham in our place. Oh, I wish I'd never come to New York! The deacon, he told me he'd keep it for me; but I wanted to put it in the bank, and now it's all gone, boo hoo!"

And the miserable youth, having despatched his cakes, was so overcome by the thought of his loss that he burst into tears.

"I say," said Dick, "dry up, and see what I've got here."

The youth no sooner saw the roll of bills, and comprehended that it was indeed his lost treasure, than from the depths of anguish he was exalted to the most ecstatic joy. He seized Dick's hand, and shook it with so much energy that our hero began to feel rather alarmed for its safety.

"'Pears to me you take my arm for a pump-handle," said he. "Couldn't you show your gratitood some other way? It's just possible I may want to use my arm ag'in some time."

The young man desisted, but invited Dick most cordially to come up and stop a week with him at his country home, assuring him that he wouldn't charge him anything for board.

"All right!" said Dick. "If you don't mind I'll bring my wife along, too. She's delicate, and the country air might do her good."

Jonathan stared at him in amazement, uncertain whether to credit the fact of his marriage. Dick walked on with Frank, leaving him in an apparent state of stupefaction, and it is possible that he has not yet settled the affair to his satisfaction.

"Now," said Frank, "I think I'll go back to the Astor House. Uncle has probably got through his business and returned."

"All right," said Dick.

The two boys walked up to Broadway, just where the tall steeple of Trinity faces the street of bankers and brokers, and walked leisurely to the hotel. When they arrived at the Astor House, Dick said, "Good-by, Frank."

"Not yet," said Frank; "I want you to come in with me."

Dick followed his young patron up the steps. Frank went to the reading-room, where, as he had thought probable, he found his uncle already arrived, and reading a copy of "The Evening Post," which he had just purchased outside.

"Well, boys," he said, looking up, "have you had a pleasant jaunt?"

"Yes, sir," said Frank. "Dick's a capital guide."

"So this is Dick," said Mr. Whitney, surveying him with a smile. "Upon my word, I should hardly have known him. I must congratulate him on his improved appearance."

"Frank's been very kind to me," said Dick, who, rough street-boy as he was, had a heart easily touched by kindness, of which he had never experienced much. "He's a tip-top fellow."

"I believe he is a good boy," said Mr. Whitney. "I hope, my lad, you will prosper and rise in the world. You know in this free country poverty in early life is no bar to a man's advancement. I haven't risen very high myself," he added, with a smile, "but have met with moderate success in life; yet there was a time when I was as poor as you."

"Were you, sir?" asked Dick, eagerly.

"Yes, my boy, I have known the time when I have been obliged to go without my dinner because I didn't have enough money to pay for it."

"How did you get up in the world?" asked Dick, anxiously.

"I entered a printing-office as an apprentice, and worked for some years. Then my eyes gave out and I was obliged to give that up. Not knowing what else to do, I went into the country, and worked on a farm. After a while I was lucky enough to invent a machine, which has brought me in a great deal of money. But there was one thing I got while I was in the printing-office which I value more than money."

"What was that, sir?"

"A taste for reading and study. During my leisure hours I improved myself by study, and acquired a large part of the knowledge which I now possess. Indeed, it was one of my books that first put me on the track of the invention, which I afterwards made. So you see, my lad, that my studious habits paid me in money, as well as in another way."

"I'm awful ignorant," said Dick, soberly.

"But you are young, and, I judge, a smart boy. If you try to learn, you can, and if you ever expect to do anything in the world, you must know something of books."

"I will," said Dick, resolutely. "I ain't always goin' to black boots for a livin'."

"All labor is respectable, my lad, and you have no cause to be ashamed of any honest business; yet when you can get something to do that promises better for your future prospects, I advise you to do so. Till then earn your living in the way you are accustomed to, avoid extravagance, and save up a little money if you can."

"Thank you for your advice," said our hero. "There ain't many that takes an interest in Ragged Dick."

"So that's your name," said Mr. Whitney. "If I judge you rightly, it won't be long before you change it. Save your money, my lad, buy books, and determine to be somebody, and you may yet fill an honorable position."

"I'll try," said Dick. "Good-night, sir."

"Wait a minute, Dick," said Frank. "Your blacking-box and old clothes are upstairs. You may want them."

"In course," said Dick. "I couldn't get along without my best clothes, and my stock in trade."

"You may go up to the room with him, Frank," said Mr. Whitney. "The clerk will give you the key. I want to see you, Dick, before you go."

"Yes, sir," said Dick.

"Where are you going to sleep to-night, Dick?" asked Frank, as they went upstairs together.

"P'r'aps at the Fifth Avenue Hotel—on the outside," said Dick.

"Haven't you any place to sleep, then?"

"I slept in a box, last night."

"In a box?"

"Yes, on Spruce Street."

"Poor fellow!" said Frank, compassionately.

"Oh, 'twas a bully bed—full of straw! I slept like a top."

"Don't you earn enough to pay for a room, Dick?"

"Yes," said Dick; "only I spend my money foolish, goin' to the Old Bowery, and Tony Pastor's, and sometimes gamblin' in Baxter Street."

"You won't gamble any more,—will you, Dick?" said Frank, laying his hand persuasively on his companion's shoulder.

"No, I won't," said Dick.

"You'll promise?"

"Yes, and I'll keep it. You're a good feller. I wish you was goin' to be in New York."

"I am going to a boarding-school in Connecticut. The name of the town is Barnton. Will you write to me, Dick?"

"My writing would look like hens' tracks," said our hero.

"Never mind. I want you to write. When you write you can tell me how to direct, and I will send you a letter."

"I wish you would," said Dick. "I wish I was more like you."

"I hope you will make a much better boy, Dick. Now we'll go in to my uncle. He wishes to see you before you go."

They went into the reading-room. Dick had wrapped up his blacking-brush in a newspaper with which Frank had supplied him, feeling that a guest of the Astor House should hardly be seen coming out of the hotel displaying such a professional sign.

"Uncle, Dick's ready to go," said Frank.

"Good-by, my lad," said Mr. Whitney. "I hope to hear good accounts of you sometime. Don't forget what I have told you. Remember that your future position depends mainly upon yourself, and that it will be high or low as you choose to make it."

He held out his hand, in which was a five-dollar bill. Dick shrunk back.

"I don't like to take it," he said. "I haven't earned it."

"Perhaps not," said Mr. Whitney; "but I give it to you because I remember my own friendless youth. I hope it may be of service to you. Sometime when you are a prosperous man, you can repay it in the form of aid to some poor boy, who is struggling upward as you are now."

"I will, sir," said Dick, manfully.

He no longer refused the money, but took it gratefully, and, bidding Frank and his uncle good-by, went out into the street. A feeling of loneliness came over him as he left the presence of Frank, for whom he had formed a strong attachment in the few hours he had known him.

CHAPTER XII

Dick Hires a Room on Mott Street

GOING out into the fresh air Dick felt the pangs of hunger. He accordingly went to a restaurant and got a substantial supper. Perhaps it was the new clothes he wore, which made him feel a little more aristocratic. At all events, instead of patronizing the cheap restaurant where he usually procured his meals, he went into the refectory attached to Lovejoy's Hotel, where the prices were higher and the company more select. In his ordinary dress, Dick would have been excluded, but now he had the appearance of a very respectable, gentlemanly boy, whose presence would not discredit any establishment. His orders were therefore received with attention by the waiter and in due time a good supper was placed before him.

"I wish I could come here every day," thought Dick. "It seems kind o' nice and 'spectable, side of the other place. There's a gent at that other table that I've shined boots for more'n once. He don't know me in my new clothes. Guess he don't know his boot-black patronizes the same establishment."

His supper over, Dick went up to the desk, and, present-ing his check, tendered in payment his five-dollar bill, as if it were one of a large number which he possessed. Receiving back his change he went out into the street.

Two questions now arose: How should he spend the eve-ning, and where should he pass the night? Yesterday, with such a sum of money in his possession, he would have an-swered both questions readily. For the evening, he would have passed it at the Old Bowery, and gone to sleep in any out-of-the-way place that offered. But he had turned over a new leaf, or resolved to do so. He meant to save his money for some useful purpose,—to aid his advancement in the world. So he could not afford the theatre. Besides, with his new clothes, he was unwilling to pass the night out of doors.

"I should spile 'em," he thought, "and that wouldn't pay."

So he determined to hunt up a room which he could oc-cupy regularly, and consider as his own, where he could sleep nights, instead of depending on boxes and old wagons for a chance shelter. This would be the first step towards re-spectability, and Dick determined to take it.

He accordingly passed through the City Hall Park, and walked leisurely up Centre Street.

He decided that it would hardly be advisable for him to seek lodgings in Fifth Avenue, although his present cash capital consisted of nearly five dollars in money, besides the valuable papers contained in his wallet. Besides, he had rea-son to doubt whether any in his line of business lived on that aristocratic street. He took his way to Mott Street, which is considerably less pretentious, and halted in front of a shabby brick lodging-house kept by a Mrs. Mooney, with whose son Tom Dick was acquainted.

Dick rang the bell, which sent back a shrill metallic re-sponse.

The door was opened by a slatternly servant, who looked at him inquiringly, and not without curiosity. It must be remembered that Dick was well dressed, and that nothing in his appearance bespoke his occupation. Being naturally a good-looking boy, he might readily be mistaken for a gentleman's son.

"Well, Queen Victoria," said Dick, "is your missus at home?"

"My name's Bridget," said the girl.

"Oh, indeed!" said Dick. "You looked so much like the queen's picter what she gave me last Christmas in exchange for mine, that I couldn't help calling you by her name."

"Oh, go along wid ye!" said Bridget. "It's makin' fun ye are."

"If you don't believe me," said Dick, gravely, "all you've got to do is to ask my partic'lar friend, the Duke of Newcastle."

"Bridget!" called a shrill voice from the basement.

"The missus is calling me," said Bridget, hurriedly. "I'll tell her ye want her."

"All right!" said Dick.

The servant descended into the lower regions, and in a short time a stout, red-faced woman appeared on the scene.

"Well, sir, what's your wish?" she asked.

"Have you got a room to let?" asked Dick.

"Is it for yourself you ask?" questioned the woman, in some surprise.

Dick answered in the affirmative.

"I haven't got any very good rooms vacant. There's a small room in the third story."

"I'd like to see it," said Dick.

"I don't know as it would be good enough for you," said the woman, with a glance at Dick's clothes.

"I ain't very partic'lar about accommodations," said our hero. "I guess I'll look at it."

Dick followed the landlady up two narrow staircases, uncarpeted and dirty, to the third landing, where he was ushered into a room about ten feet square. It could not be considered a very desirable apartment. It had once been covered with an oilcloth carpet, but this was now very ragged, and looked worse than none. There was a single bed in the corner, covered with an indiscriminate heap of bed-clothing, rumpled and not over-clean. There was a bureau, with the veneering scratched and in some parts stripped off, and a small glass, eight inches by ten, cracked across the middle; also two chairs in rather a disjointed condition. Judging from Dick's appearance, Mrs. Mooney thought he would turn from it in disdain.

But it must be remembered that Dick's past experience had not been of a character to make him fastidious. In comparison with a box, or an empty wagon, even this little room seemed comfortable. He decided to hire it if the rent proved reasonable.

"Well, what's the tax?" asked Dick.

"I ought to have a dollar a week," said Mrs. Mooney, hesitatingly.

"Say seventy-five cents, and I'll take it," said Dick.

"Every week in advance?"

"Yes."

"Well, as times is hard, and I can't afford to keep it empty, you may have it. When will you come?"

"To-night," said Dick.

"It ain't lookin' very neat. I don't know as I can fix it up to-night."

"Well, I'll sleep here to-night, and you can fix it up to-morrow."

"I hope you'll excuse the looks. I'm a lone woman, and my help is so shiftless, I have to look after everything myself; so I can't keep things as straight as I want to."

"All right!" said Dick.

"Can you pay me the first week in advance?" asked the landlady, cautiously.

Dick responded by drawing seventy-five cents from his pocket, and placing it in her hand.

"What's your business, sir, if I may inquire?" said Mrs. Mooney.

"Oh, I'm professional!" said Dick.

"Indeed!" said the landlady, who did not feel much enlightened by this answer.

"How's Tom?" asked Dick.

"Do you know my Tom?" said Mrs. Mooney in surprise. "He's gone to sea,—to Californy. He went last week."

"Did he?" said Dick. "Yes, I knew him."

Mrs. Mooney looked upon her new lodger with increased favor, on finding that he was acquainted with her son, who, by the way, was one of the worst young scamps in Mott Street, which is saying considerable.

"I'll bring over my baggage from the Astor House this evening," said Dick in a tone of importance.

"From the Astor House!" repeated Mrs. Mooney, in fresh amazement.

"Yes, I've been stoppin' there a short time with some friends," said Dick.

Mrs. Mooney might be excused for a little amazement at finding that a guest from the Astor House was about to become one of her lodgers—such transfers not being common.

"Did you say you was purfessional?" she asked.

"Yes, ma'am," said Dick, politely.

"You ain't a—a—" Mrs. Mooney paused, uncertain what conjecture to hazard.

"Oh, no, nothing of the sort," said Dick, promptly. "How could you think so, Mrs. Mooney?"

"No offense, sir," said the landlady, more perplexed than ever.

"Certainly not," said our hero. "But you must excuse me now, Mrs. Mooney, as I have business of great importance to attend to."

"You'll come round this evening?"

Dick answered in the affirmative, and turned away.

"I wonder what he is!" thought the landlady, following him with her eyes as he crossed the street. "He's got good clothes on, but he don't seem very particular about his room. Well, I've got all my rooms full now. That's one comfort."

Dick felt more comfortable now that he had taken the decisive step of hiring a lodging, and paying a week's rent in advance. For seven nights he was sure of a shelter and a bed to sleep in. The thought was a pleasant one to our young vagrant, who hitherto had seldom known when he rose in the morning where he should find a resting-place at night.

"I must bring my traps round," said Dick to himself. "I guess I'll go to bed early to-night. It'll feel kinder good to sleep in a reg'lar bed. Boxes is rather hard to the back, and ain't comfortable in case of rain. I wonder what Johnny Nolan would say if he knew I'd got a room of my own."

CHAPTER XIII

Micky Maguire

ABOUT nine o'clock Dick sought his new lodgings. In his hands he carried his professional wardrobe, namely, the clothes which he had worn at the commencement of the day, and the implements of his business. These he stowed away in the bureau drawers, and by the light of a flickering candle took off his clothes and went to bed. Dick had a good digestion and a reasonably good conscience; consequently he was a good sleeper. Perhaps, too, the soft feather bed conduced to slumber. At any rate his eyes were soon closed, and he did not awake until half-past six the next morning.

He lifted himself on his elbow, and stared around him in transient bewilderment.

"Blest if I hadn't forgot where I was," he said to himself. "So this is my room, is it? Well, it seems kind of 'spectable to have a room and a bed to sleep in. I'd orter be able to afford seventy-five cents a week. I've throwed away more money than that in one evenin'. There ain't no reason why I shouldn't live 'spectable. I wish I knowed as much as Frank.

He's a tip-top feller. Nobody ever cared enough for me before to give me good advice. It was kicks, and cuffs, and swearin' at me all the time. I'd like to show him I can do something."

While Dick was indulging in these reflections, he had risen from bed, and, finding an accession to the furniture of his room, in the shape of an ancient wash-stand bearing a cracked bowl and broken pitcher, indulged himself in the rather unusual ceremony of a good wash. On the whole, Dick preferred to be clean, but it was not always easy to gratify his desire. Lodging in the street as he had been accustomed to do, he had had no opportunity to perform his toilet in the customary manner. Even now he found himself unable to arrange his dishevelled locks, having neither comb nor brush. He determined to purchase a comb, at least, as soon as possible, and a brush too, if he could get one cheap. Meanwhile he combed his hair with his fingers as well as he could, though the result was not quite so satisfactory as it might have been.

A question now came up for consideration. For the first time in his life Dick possessed two suits of clothes. Should he put on the clothes Frank had given him, or resume his old rags?

Now, twenty-four hours before, at the time Dick was introduced to the reader's notice, no one could have been less fastidious as to his clothing than he. Indeed, he had rather a contempt for good clothes, or at least he thought so. But now, as he surveyed the ragged and dirty coat and the patched pants, Dick felt ashamed of them. He was unwilling to appear in the streets with them. Yet, if he went to work in his new suit, he was in danger of spoiling it, and he might not have it in his power to purchase a new one. Economy dictated a return to the old garments. Dick tried them on, and surveyed himself in the cracked glass; but the reflection did not please him.

"They don't look 'spectable," he decided; and forthwith taking them off again, he put on the new suit of the day before.

"I must try to earn a little more," he thought, "to pay for my room, and to buy some new clo'es when these is wore out."

He opened the door of his chamber, and went downstairs and into the street, carrying his blacking-box with him.

It was Dick's custom to commence his business before breakfast; generally it must be owned, because he began the day penniless, and must earn his meal before he ate it. To-day it was different. He had four dollars left in his pocket-book; but this he had previously determined not to touch. In fact he had formed the ambitious design of starting an account at a savings bank, in order to have something to fall back upon in case of sickness or any other emergency, or at any rate as a reserve fund to expend in clothing or other necessary articles when he required them. Hitherto he had been content to live on from day to day without a penny ahead; but the new vision of respectability which now floated before Dick's mind, owing to his recent acquaintance with Frank, was beginning to exercise a powerful effect upon him.

In Dick's profession as in others there are lucky days, when everything seems to flow prosperously. As if to encourage him in his new-born resolution, our hero obtained no less than six jobs in the course of an hour and a half. This gave him sixty cents, quite abundant to purchase his breakfast, and a comb besides. His exertions made him hungry, and entering a small eating-house he ordered a cup of coffee and a beefsteak. To this he added a couple of rolls. This was quite a luxurious breakfast for Dick, and more expensive than he was accustomed to indulge himself with. To gratify the curiosity of my young readers, I will put down the items with their cost—

Coffee, ...	5 cts.
Beefsteak, ...	15
A couple of rolls, ...	5
	<u>25 cts.</u>

It will thus be seen that our hero had expended nearly one-half of his morning's earnings. Some days he had been compelled to breakfast on five cents, and then he was forced to content himself with a couple of apples, or cakes. But a good breakfast is a good preparation for a busy day, and Dick sallied forth from the restaurant lively and alert, ready to do a good stroke of business.

Dick's change of costume was liable to lead to one result of which he had not thought. His brother boot-blacks might think he had grown aristocratic, and was putting on airs,— that, in fact, he was getting above his business, and desirous to outshine his associates. Dick had not dreamed of this, because in fact, in spite of his new-born ambition, he entertained no such feelings. There was nothing of what boys call "big-feeling" about him. He was a thorough democrat, using the word not politically, but in its proper sense, and was disposed to fraternize with all whom he styled "good fellows," without regard to their position. It may seem a little unnecessary to some of my readers to make this explanation; but they must remember that pride and "big-feeling" are confined to no age or class, but may be found in boys as well as men, and in boot-blacks as well as those of a higher rank.

The morning being a busy time with the boot-blacks, Dick's changed appearance had not as yet attracted much attention. But when business slackened a little, our hero was destined to be reminded of it.

Among the down-town boot-blacks was one hailing from the Five Points,—a stout, red-haired, freckled-faced boy of fourteen, bearing the name of Micky Maguire. This boy, by his boldness and recklessness, as well as by his personal strength, which was considerable, had acquired an ascendency among his fellow professionals, and had a gang of subservient followers, whom he led on to acts of ruffianism, not unfrequently terminating in a month or two at Blackwell's Island. Micky himself had served two terms there; but the confinement appeared to have had very little effect in amending his conduct, except, perhaps, in making him a little more cautious about an encounter with the "copps," as the members of the city police are, for some unknown reason, styled among the Five-Point boys.

Now Micky was proud of his strength, and of the position of leader which it had secured him. Moreover he was democratic in his tastes, and had a jealous hatred of those who wore good clothes and kept their faces clean. He called it putting on airs, and resented the implied superiority. If he had been fifteen years older, and had a trifle more education, he would have interested himself in politics, and been prominent at ward meetings, and a terror to respectable voters on election day. As it was, he contented himself with being the leader of a gang of young ruffians, over whom he wielded a despotic power.

Now it is only justice to Dick to say that, so far as wearing good clothes was concerned, he had never hitherto offended the eyes of Micky Maguire. Indeed, they generally looked as if they patronized the same clothing establishment. On this particular morning it chanced that Micky had not been very fortunate in a business way, and, as a natural consequence, his temper, never very amiable, was somewhat ruffled by the fact. He had had a very frugal breakfast,—not because he felt abstemious, but owing to the low state of his finances. He was walking along with one of his particular friends, a boy nick-named Limpy Jim, so called from a slight peculiarity in his walk, when all at once he espied our friend Dick in his new suit.

"My eyes!" he exclaimed, in astonishment; "Jim, just

look at Ragged Dick. He's come into a fortun', and turned gentleman. See his new clothes."

"So he has," said Jim. "Where'd he get 'em, I wonder?"

"Hooked 'em, p'r'aps. Let's go and stir him up a little. We don't want no gentlemen on our beat. So he's puttin' on airs,—is he? I'll give him a lesson."

So saying the two boys walked up to our hero, who had not observed them, his back being turned, and Micky Maguire gave him a smart slap on the shoulder.

Dick turned round quickly.

CHAPTER XIV

A Battle and a Victory

"WHAT'S that for?" demanded Dick, turning round to see who had struck him.

"You're gettin' mighty fine!" said Micky Maguire, surveying Dick's new clothes with a scornful air.

There was something in his words and tone, which Dick, who was disposed to stand up for his dignity, did not at all relish.

"Well, what's the odds if I am?" he retorted. "Does it hurt you any?"

"See him put on airs, Jim," said Micky, turning to his companion. "Where'd you get them clo'es?"

"Never mind where I got 'em. Maybe the Prince of Wales gave 'em to me."

"Hear him, now, Jim," said Micky. "Most likely he stole 'em."

"Stealin' ain't in *my* line."

It might have been unconscious the emphasis which Dick placed on the word "my." At any rate Micky chose to take offense.

"Do you mean to say *I* steal?" he demanded, doubling up his fist, and advancing towards Dick in a threatening manner.

"I don't say anything about it," answered Dick, by no means alarmed at this hostile demonstration. "I know you've been to the island twice. P'r'aps 'twas to make a visit along of the Mayor and Aldermen. Maybe you was a innocent victim of oppression. I ain't a-goin' to say."

Mickey's freckled face grew red with wrath, for Dick had only stated the truth.

"Do you mean to insult me?" he demanded, shaking the fist already doubled up in Dick's face. "Maybe you want a lickin'?"

"I ain't partic'larly anxious to get one," said Dick, coolly. "They don't agree with my constitution which is nat'rally delicate. I'd rather have a good dinner than a lickin' any time."

"You're afraid," sneered Micky. "Isn't he, Jim?"

"In course he is."

"P'r'aps I am," said Dick, composedly, "but it don't trouble me much."

"Do you want to fight?" demanded Micky, encouraged by Dick's quietness, fancying he was afraid to encounter him.

"No, I don't," said Dick. "I ain't fond of fightin'. It's a very good amusement, and very bad for the complexion, 'specially for the eyes and nose, which is apt to run red, white, and blue."

Micky misunderstood Dick, and judged from the tenor of his speech that he would be an easy victim. As he knew, Dick very seldom was concerned in any street fight,—not from cowardice, as he imagined—but because he had too much good sense to do so. Being quarrelsome, like all bullies, and supposing that he was more than a match for our hero, being about two inches taller, he could no longer resist an inclination to assault him, and tried to plant a blow in

Dick's face which would have hurt him considerably if he had not drawn back just in time.

Now, though Dick was far from quarrelsome, he was ready to defend himself on all occasions, and it was too much to expect that he would stand quiet and allow himself to be beaten.

He dropped his blacking-box on the instant, and returned Micky's blow with such good effect that the young bully staggered back, and would have fallen, if he had not been propped up by his confederate, Limpy Jim.

"Go in, Micky!" shouted the latter, who was rather a coward on his own account, but liked to see others fight. "Polish him off, that's a good feller."

Micky was now boiling over with rage and fury, and required no urging. He was fully determined to make a terrible example of poor Dick. He threw himself upon him, and strove to bear him to the ground; but Dick, avoiding a close hug, in which he might possibly have got the worst of it, by an adroit movement, tripped up his antagonist, and stretched him on the sidewalk.

"Hit him, Jim!" exclaimed Micky, furiously.

Limpy Jim did not seem inclined to obey orders. There was a quiet strength and coolness about Dick, which alarmed him. He preferred that Micky should incur all the risks of battle, and accordingly set himself to raising his fallen comrade.

"Come, Micky," said Dick, quietly, "you'd better give it up. I wouldn't have touched you if you hadn't hit me first. I don't want to fight. It's low business."

"You're afraid of hurtin' your clo'es," said Micky, with a sneer.

"Maybe I am," said Dick. "I hope I haven't hurt yours."

Micky's answer to this was another attack, as violent and impetuous as the first. But his fury was in the way. He struck wildly, not measuring his blows, and Dick had no difficulty in turning aside, so that his antagonist's blow fell upon the empty air, and his momentum was such that he nearly fell forward headlong. Dick might readily have taken advantage of his unsteadiness, and knocked him down; but he was not vindictive, and chose to act on the defensive, except when he could not avoid it.

Recovering himself, Micky saw that Dick was a more formidable antagonist than he had supposed, and was meditating another assault, better planned, which by its impetuosity might bear our hero to the ground. But there was an unlooked-for interference.

"Look out for the 'copp,' " said Jim, in a low voice.

Micky turned round and saw a tall policeman heading towards him, and thought it might be prudent to suspend hostilities. He accordingly picked up his blacking-box, and hitching up his pants, walked off, attended by Limpy Jim.

"What's that chap been doing?" asked the policeman of Dick.

"He was amoosin' himself by pitchin' into me," replied Dick.

"What for?"

"He didn't like it 'cause I patronized a different tailor from him."

"Well, it seems to me you *are* dressed pretty smart for a boot-black," said the policeman.

"I wish I wasn't a boot-black," said Dick.

"Never mind, my lad. It's an honest business," said the policeman, who was a sensible man and a worthy citizen. "It's an honest business. Stick to it till you get something better."

"I mean to," said Dick. "It ain't easy to get out of it, as the prisoner remarked, when he was asked how he liked his residence."

"I hope you don't speak from experience."

"No," said Dick; "I don't mean to get into prison if I can help it."

"Do you see that gentleman over there?" asked the officer, pointing to a well-dressed man who was walking on the other side of the street.

"Yes."

"Well, he was once a newsboy."

"And what is he now?"

"He keeps a bookstore, and is quite prosperous."

Dick looked at the gentleman with interest, wondering if he should look as respectable when he was a grown man.

It will be seen that Dick was getting ambitious. Hitherto he had thought very little of the future, but was content to get along as he could, dining as well as his means would allow, and spending the evenings in the pit of the Old Bowery, eating peanuts between the acts if he was prosperous, and if unlucky supping on dry bread or an apple, and sleeping in an old box or a wagon. Now, for the first time, he began to reflect that he could not black boots all his life. In seven years he would be a man, and, since his meeting with Frank, he felt he would like to be a respectable man. He could see and appreciate the difference between Frank and such a boy as Micky Maguire, and it was not strange that he preferred the society of the former.

In the course of the next morning, in pursuance of his new resolutions for the future, he called at a savings bank, and held out four dollars in bills besides another dollar in change. There was a high railing, and a number of clerks busily writing at desks behind it. Dick, never having been in a bank before, did not know where to go. He went, by mistake, to the desk where money was paid out.

"Where's your book?" asked the clerk.

"I haven't got any."

"Have you any money deposited here?"

"No, sir, I want to leave some here."

"Then go to the next desk."

Dick followed directions, and presented himself before

an elderly man with gray hair, who looked at him over the rims of his spectacles.

"I want you to keep that for me," said Dick, awkwardly emptying his money out on the desk.

"How much is there?"

"Five dollars."

"Have you got an account here?"

"No, sir."

"Of course you can write?"

The "of course" was said on account of Dick's neat dress.

"Have I got to do any writing?" asked our hero, a little embarrassed.

"We want you to sign your name in this book," and the old gentleman shoved round a large folio volume containing the names of depositors.

Dick surveyed the book with some awe.

"I ain't much on writin'," he said.

"Very well, write as well as you can."

The pen was put into Dick's hand, and, after dipping it in the inkstand, he succeeded after a hard effort, accompanied by many contortions of the face, in inscribing upon the book of the bank the name

DICK HUNTER.

"Dick!—that means Richard, I suppose," said the bank officer, who had some difficulty in making out the signature.

"No; Ragged Dick is what folks call me."

"You don't look very ragged."

"No, I've left my rags to home. They might get wore out if I used 'em too common."

"Well, my lad, I'll make out a book in the name of Dick Hunter, since you seem to prefer Dick to Richard. I hope you will save up your money and deposit more with us."

Our hero took his bank-book, and gazed on the entry "Five Dollars" with a new sense of importance. He had been accustomed to joke about Erie shares, but now, for the first time, he felt himself a capitalist; on a small scale, to be sure, but still it was no small thing for Dick to have five dollars which he could call his own. He firmly determined that he would lay by every cent he could spare from his earnings towards the fund he hoped to accumulate.

But Dick was too sensible not to know that there was something more than money needed to win a respectable position in the world. He felt that he was very ignorant. Of reading and writing he only knew the rudiments, and that, with a slight acquaintance with arithmetic, was all he did know of books. Dick knew he must study hard, and he dreaded it. He looked upon learning as attended with greater difficulties than it really possesses. But Dick had good pluck. He meant to learn, nevertheless, and resolved to buy a book with his first spare earnings.

When Dick went home at night he locked up his bank-book in one of the drawers of the bureau. It was wonderful how much more independent he felt whenever he reflected upon the contents of that drawer, and with what an important air of joint ownership he regarded the bank building in which his small savings were deposited.

CHAPTER XV

Dick Secures a Tutor

THE next morning Dick was unusually successful, having plenty to do, and receiving for one job twenty-five cents,— the gentleman refusing to take change. Then flashed upon Dick's mind the thought that he had not yet returned the change due to the gentleman whose boots he had blacked on the morning of his introduction to the reader.

"What'll he think of me?" said Dick to himself. "I hope he won't think I'm mean enough to keep the money."

Now Dick was scrupulously honest, and though the temptation to be otherwise had often been strong, he had always resisted it. He was not willing on any account to keep money which did not belong to him, and he immediately started for 125 Fulton Street (the address which had been given him) where he found Mr. Greyson's name on the door of an office on the first floor.

The door being open, Dick walked in.

"Is Mr. Greyson in?" he asked of a clerk who sat on a high stool before a desk.

"Not just now. He'll be in soon. Will you wait?"

"Yes," said Dick.

"Very well; take a seat then."

Dick sat down and took up the morning "Tribune," but presently came to a word of four syllables, which he pronounced to himself a "sticker," and laid it down. But he had not long to wait, for five minutes later Mr. Greyson entered.

"Did you wish to speak to me, my lad?" said he to Dick, whom in his new clothes he did not recognize.

"Yes, sir," said Dick. "I owe you some money."

"Indeed!" said Mr. Greyson, pleasantly; "that's an agreeable surprise. I didn't know but you had come for some. So you are a debtor of mine, and not a creditor?"

"I believe that's right," said Dick, drawing fifteen cents from his pocket, and placing in Mr. Greyson's hand.

"Fifteen cents!" repeated he, in some surprise. "How do you happen to be indebted to me in that amount?"

"You gave me a quarter for a-shinin' your boots, yesterday mornin', and couldn't wait for the change. I meant to have brought it before, but I forgot all about it till this mornin'."

"It had quite slipped my mind also. But you don't look like the boy I employed. If I remember rightly he wasn't as well dressed as you."

"No," said Dick. "I was dressed for a party, then, but the clo'es was too well ventilated to be comfortable in cold weather."

"You're an honest boy," said Mr. Greyson. "Who taught you to be honest?"

"Nobody," said Dick. "But it's mean to cheat and steal. I've always knowed that."

"Then you've got ahead of some of our business men. Do you read the Bible?"

"No," said Dick. "I've heard it's a good book, but I don't know much about it."

"You ought to go to some Sunday school. Would you be willing?"

"Yes," said Dick, promptly. "I want to grow up 'spect-able. But I don't know where to go."

"Then I'll tell you. The church I attend is at the corner of Fifth Avenue and Twenty-first Street."

"I've seen it," said Dick.

"I have a class in the Sunday school there. If you'll come next Sunday, I'll take you into my class, and do what I can to help you."

"Thank you," said Dick, "but p'r'aps you'll get tired of teaching me. I'm awful ignorant."

"No, my lad," said Mr. Greyson, kindly. "You evidently have some good principles to start with, as you have shown by your scorn of dishonesty. I shall hope good things of you in the future."

"Well, Dick," said our hero, apostrophizing himself, as he left the office; "you're gettin' up in the world. You've got money invested, and are goin' to attend church, by particular invitation, on Fifth Avenue. I shouldn't wonder much if you should find cards, when you get home, from the Mayor, re-questin' the honor of your company to dinner, along with other distinguished guests."

Dick felt in very good spirits. He seemed to be emerging from the world in which he had hitherto lived, into a new atmosphere of respectability, and the change seemed very pleasant to him.

At six o'clock Dick went into a restaurant on Chatham Street, and got a comfortable supper. He had been so suc-cessful during the day that, after paying for this, he still had ninety cents left. While he was despatching his supper, an-other boy came in, smaller and slighter than Dick, and sat down beside him. Dick recognized him as a boy who three months before had entered the ranks of the boot-blacks, but who, from a natural timidity, had not been able to earn much. He was ill-fitted for the coarse companionship of the street-boys, and shrank from the rude jokes of his present associates. Dick had never troubled him; for our hero had a certain chivalrous feeling which would not allow him to bully or disturb a younger and weaker boy than himself.

"How are you, Fosdick?" said Dick, as the other seated himself.

"Pretty well," said Fosdick. "I suppose you're all right."

"Oh, yes, I'm right side up with care. I've been havin' a bully supper. What are you goin' to have?"

"Some bread and butter."

"Why don't you get a cup o' coffee?"

"Why," said Fosdick, reluctantly, "I haven't got money enough to-night."

"Never mind," said Dick; "I'm in luck to-day. I'll stand treat."

"That's kind in you," said Fosdick, gratefully.

"Oh, never mind that," said Dick.

Accordingly he ordered a cup of coffee, and a plate of beefsteak, and was gratified to see that his young companion partook of both with evident relish. When the repast was over, the boys went out into the street together, Dick passing at the desk to settle for both suppers.

"Where are you going to sleep to-night, Fosdick?" asked Dick, as they stood on the sidewalk.

"I don't know," said Fosdick, a little sadly. "In some door-way, I expect. But I'm afraid the police will find me out, and make me move on."

"I'll tell you what," said Dick, "you must go home with me. I guess my bed will hold two."

"Have you got a room?" asked the other, in surprise.

"Yes," said Dick, rather proudly, and with a little excusable exultation. "I've got a room over on Mott Street; there I can receive my friends. That'll be better than sleepin' in a door-way,—won't it?"

"Yes, indeed it will," said Fosdick. "How lucky I was to come across you! It comes hard to me living as I do. When my father was alive I had every comfort."

"That's more'n I ever had," said Dick. "But I'm goin' to try to live comfortable now. Is your father dead?"

"Yes," said Fosdick, sadly. "He was a printer; but he was drowned one dark night from a Fulton ferry-boat, and, as I had no relations in the city, and no money, I was obliged to go to work as quick as I could. But I don't get on very well."

"Didn't you have no brothers nor sisters?" asked Dick.

"No," said Fosdick; "father and I used to live alone. He was always so much company to me that I feel very lonesome without him. There's a man out West somewhere that owes him two thousand dollars. He used to live in the city, and father lent him all his money to help him go into business; but he failed, or pretended to, and went off. If father hadn't lost that money he would have left me well off; but no money would have made up his loss to me."

"What's the man's name that went off with your father's money?"

"His name is Hiram Bates."

"P'r'aps you'll get the money again, sometime."

"There isn't much chance of it," said Fosdick. "I'd sell out my chances of that for five dollars."

"Maybe I'll buy you out some time," said Dick. "Now, come round and see what sort of a room I've got. I used to go to the theatre evenings, when I had money; but now I'd rather go to bed early, and have a good sleep."

"I don't care much about theatres," said Fosdick. "Father didn't use to let me go very often. He said it wasn't good for boys."

"I like to go to the Old Bowery sometimes. They have tip-top plays there. Can you read and write well?" he asked, as a sudden thought came to him.

"Yes," said Fosdick. "Father always kept me at school

when he was alive, and I stood pretty well in my classes. I was expecting to enter at the Free Academy* next year."

"Then I'll tell you what," said Dick; "I'll make a bargain with you. I can't read much more'n a pig; and my writin' looks like hens' tracks. I don't want to grow up knowin' no more'n a four-year-old boy. If you'll teach me readin' and writin' evenin's, you shall sleep in my room every night. That'll be better'n door-steps or old boxes, where I've slept many a time."

"Are you in earnest?" said Fosdick, his face lighting up hopefully.

"In course I am," said Dick. "It's fashionable for young gentlemen to have private tootors to introduce 'em into the flower-beds of literatoor and science, and why should't I foller the fashion? You shall be my perfessor; only you must promise not to be very hard if my writin' looks like a rail-fence or a bender."

"I'll try not to be too severe," said Fosdick, laughing. "I shall be thankful for such a chance to get a place to sleep. Have you got anything to read out of?"

"No," said Dick. "My extensive and well-selected library was lost overboard in a storm, when I was sailin' from the Sandwich Islands to the desert of Sahara. But I'll buy a paper. That'll do me a long time."

Accordingly Dick stopped at a paper-stand, and bought a copy of a weekly paper, filled with the usual variety of reading matter,—stories, sketches, poems, etc.

They soon arrived at Dick's lodging-house. Our hero, procuring a lamp from the landlady, led the way into his apartment, which he entered with the proud air of a proprietor.

"Well, how do you like it, Fosdick?" he asked, complacently.

* Now the college of the city of New York.

The time was when Fosdick would have thought it untidy and not particularly attractive. But he had served a severe apprenticeship in the streets, and it was pleasant to feel himself under shelter, and he was not disposed to be critical.

"It looks very comfortable, Dick," he said.

"The bed ain't very large," said Dick; "but I guess we can get along."

"Oh, yes," said Fosdick, cheerfully. "I don't take up much room."

"Then that's all right. There's two chairs, you see, one for you and one for me. In case the mayor comes in to spend the evenin' socially, he can sit on the bed."

The boys seated themselves, and five minutes later, under the guidance of his young tutor, Dick had commenced his studies.

CHAPTER XVI

The First Lesson

FORTUNATELY for Dick, his young tutor was well qualified to instruct him. Henry Fosdick, though only twelve years old, knew as much as many boys of fourteen. He had always been studious and ambitious to excel. His father, being a printer, employed in an office where books were printed, often brought home new books in sheets, which Henry was always glad to read. Mr. Fosdick had been, besides, a subscriber to the Mechanics' Apprentices' Library, which contains many thousands of well-selected and instructive books. Thus Henry had acquired an amount of general information, unusual in a boy of his age. Perhaps he had devoted too much time to study, for he was not naturally robust. All this, however, fitted him admirably for the office to which Dick had appointed him,—that of his private instructor.

The two boys drew up their chairs to the rickety table, and spread out the paper before them.

"The exercises generally commence with ringing the bell," said Dick; "but as I ain't got none, we'll have to do without."

"And the teacher is generally provided with a rod," said Fosdick. "Isn't there a poker handy, that I can use in case my scholar doesn't behave well?"

"'Taint lawful to use fire-arms," said Dick.

"Now, Dick," said Fosdick, "before we begin, I must find out how much you already know. Can you read any?"

"Not enough to hurt me," said Dick. "All I know about readin' you could put in a nutshell, and there'd be room left for a small family."

"I suppose you know your letters?"

"Yes," said Dick, "I know 'em all, but not intimately. I guess I can call 'em all by name."

"Where did you learn them? Did you ever go to school?"

"Yes; I went two days."

"Why did you stop?"

"It didn't agree with my constitution."

"You don't look very delicate," said Fosdick.

"No," said Dick, "I ain't troubled much that way; but I found lickin's didn't agree with me."

"Did you get punished?"

"Awful," said Dick.

"What for?"

"For indulgin' in a little harmless amoosement," said Dick. "You see the boy that was sittin' next to me fell asleep, which I considered improper in school-time; so I thought I'd help the teacher a little by wakin' him up. So I took a pin and stuck into him; but I guess it went a little too far, for he screeched awful. The teacher found out what it was that made him holler, and whipped me with a ruler till I was black and blue. I thought 'twas about time to take a vacation; so that's the last time I went to school."

"You didn't learn to read in that time, of course?"

"No," said Dick; "but I was a newsboy a little while; so I learned a little, just so's to find out what the news was. Sometimes I didn't read straight and called the wrong news.

One mornin' I asked another boy what the paper said, and he told me the King of Africa was dead. I thought it was all right till folks began to laugh."

"Well, Dick, if you'll only study well, you won't be liable to make such mistakes."

"I hope so," said Dick. "My friend Horace Greeley told me the other day that he'd get me to take his place now and then when he was off makin' speeches if my edication hadn't been neglected."

"I must find a good piece for you to begin on," said Fosdick, looking over the paper.

"Find an easy one," said Dick, "with words of one story."

Fosdick at length found a piece which he thought would answer. He discovered on trial that Dick had not exaggerated his deficiencies. Words of two syllables he seldom pronounced right, and was much surprised when he was told how "through" was sounded.

"Seems to me it's throwin' away letters to use all them," he said.

"How would you spell it?" asked his young teacher.

"T-h-r-u," said Dick.

"Well," said Fosdick, "there's a good many other words that are spelt with more letters than they need to have. But it's the fashion, and we must follow it."

But if Dick was ignorant, he was quick, and had an excellent capacity. Moreover he had a perseverance, and was not easily discouraged. He had made up his mind he must know more, and was not disposed to complain of the difficulty of his task. Fosdick had occasion to laugh more than once at his ludicrous mistakes; but Dick laughed too, and on the whole both were quite interested in the lesson.

At the end of an hour and a half the boys stopped for the evening.

"You're learning fast, Dick," said Fosdick. "At this rate you will soon learn to read well."

"Will I?" asked Dick with an expression of satisfaction. "I'm glad of that. I don't want to be ignorant. I didn't use to care, but I do now. I want to grow up 'spectable."

"So do I, Dick. We will both help each other, and I am sure we can accomplish something. But I am beginning to feel sleepy."

"So am I," said Dick. "Them hard words make my head ache. I wonder who made 'em all?"

"That's more than I can tell. I suppose you've seen a dictionary."

"That's another of 'em. No, I can't say I have, though I may have seen him in the street without knowin' him."

"A dictionary is a book containing all the words in the language."

"How many are there?"

"I don't rightly know; but I think there are about fifty thousand."

"It's a pretty large family," said Dick. "Have I got to learn 'em all?"

"That will not be necessary. There are a large number which you would never find occasion to use."

"I'm glad of that," said Dick; "for I don't expect to live to be more'n a hundred, and by that time I wouldn't be more'n half through."

By this time the flickering lamp gave a decided hint to the boys that unless they made haste they would have to undress in the dark. They accordingly drew off their clothes, and Dick jumped into bed. But Fosdick, before doing so, knelt down by the side of the bed, and said a short prayer.

"What's that for?" asked Dick, curiously.

"I was saying my prayers," said Fosdick, as he rose from his knees. "Don't you ever do it?"

"No," said Dick. "Nobody ever taught me."

"Then I'll teach you. Shall I?"

"I don't know," said Dick, dubiously. "What's the good?"

Fosdick explained as well as he could, and perhaps his simple explanation was better adapted to Dick's comprehension than one from an older person would have been. Dick felt more free to ask questions, and the example of his new friend, for whom he was beginning to feel a warm attachment, had considerable effect upon him. When, therefore, Fosdick asked again if he should teach him a prayer, Dick consented, and his young bedfellow did so. Dick was not naturally irreligious. If he had lived without a knowledge of God and of religious things, it was scarcely to be wondered at in a lad who, from an early age, had been thrown upon his own exertions for the means of living, with no one to care for him or give him good advice. But he was so far good that he could appreciate goodness in others, and this it was that had drawn him to Frank in the first place, and now to Henry Fosdick. He did not, therefore, attempt to ridicule his companion, as some boys better brought up might have done, but was willing to follow his example in what something told him was right. Our young hero had taken an important step towards securing that genuine respectability which he was ambitious to attain.

Weary with the day's work, and Dick perhaps still more fatigued by the unusual mental effort he had made, the boys soon sank into a deep and peaceful slumber, from which they did not awaken till six o'clock the next morning. Before going out Dick sought Mrs. Mooney, and spoke to her on the subject of taking Fosdick as a room-mate. He found that she had no objection, provided he would allow her twenty-five cents a week extra, in consideration of the extra trouble which his companion might be expected to make. To this Dick assented, and the arrangement was definitely concluded.

This over, the two boys went out and took stations near each other. Dick had more of a business turn than Henry, and less shrinking from publicity, so that his earnings were greater. But he had undertaken to pay the entire expenses of the room, and needed to earn more. Sometimes, when two customers presented themselves at the same time, he was able to direct one to his friend. So at the end of the week both boys found themselves with surplus earnings. Dick had the satisfaction of adding two dollars and a half to his deposits in the savings bank, and Fosdick commenced an account by depositing seventy-five cents.

On Sunday morning Dick bethought himself of his promise to Mr. Greyson to come to the church on Fifth Avenue. To tell the truth, Dick recalled it with some regret. He had never been inside a church since he could remember, and he was not much attracted by the invitation he had received. But Henry, finding him wavering, urged him to go, and offered to go with him. Dick gladly accepted the offer, feeling that he required some one to lend him countenance under such unusual circumstances.

Dick dressed himself with scrupulous care, giving his shoes a "shine" so brilliant that it did him great credit in a professional point of view, and endeavored to clean his hands thoroughly; but, in spite of all he could do, they were not so white as if his business had been of a different character.

Having fully completed his preparations, he descended into the street, and, with Henry by his side, crossed over to Broadway.

The boys pursued their way up Broadway, which on Sunday presents a striking contrast in its quietness to the noise and confusion of ordinary weekdays, as far as Union Square then turned down Fourteenth Street, which brought them to Fifth Avenue.

"Suppose we dine at Delmonico's," said Fosdick, looking towards that famous restaurant.

"I'd have to sell some of my Erie shares," said Dick.

A short walk now brought them to the church of which

mention has already been made. They stood outside, a little abashed, watching the fashionably attired people who were entering, and were feeling a little undecided as to whether they had better enter also, when Dick felt a light touch upon his shoulder.

Turning round, he met the smiling glance of Mr. Greyson.

"So, my young friend, you have kept your promise," he said. "And whom have you brought with you?"

"A friend of mine," said Dick. "His name is Henry Fosdick."

"I am glad you have brought him. Now follow me, and I will give you seats."

CHAPTER XVII

~~~

Dick's First Appearance
in Society

It was the hour for morning service. The boys followed Mr. Greyson into the handsome church, and were assigned seats in his own pew.

There were two persons already seated in it,—a good-looking lady of middle age, and a pretty little girl of nine. They were Mrs. Greyson and her only daughter, Ida. They looked pleasantly at the boys as they entered, smiling a welcome to them.

The morning service commenced. It must be acknowledged that Dick felt rather awkward. It was an unusual place for him, and it need not be wondered at that he felt like a cat in a strange garret. He would not have known when to rise if he had not taken notice of what the rest of the audience did, and followed their example. He was sitting next to Ida and as it was the first time he had ever been near so well-dressed a young lady, he naturally felt bashful. When the hymns were announced, Ida found the place, and offered a hymn-book to our hero. Dick took it awkwardly, but his studies had not yet been pursued far enough for him to read the words readily. However, he resolved to keep up appearances, and kept his eyes fixed steadily on the hymn-book.

At length the service was over. The people began to file slowly out of church, and among them, of course, Mr. Greyson's family and the two boys. It seemed very strange to Dick to find himself in such different companionship from what he had been accustomed, and he could not help thinking, "Wonder what Johnny Nolan 'ould say if he could see me now!"

But Johnny's business engagements did not often summon him to Fifth Avenue, and Dick was not likely to be seen by any of his friends in the lower part of the city.

"We have our Sunday school in the afternoon," said Mr. Greyson. "I suppose you live at some distance from here?"

"In Mott Street, sir," answered Dick.

"That is too far to go and return. Suppose you and your friend come and dine with us, and then we can come here together in the afternoon."

Dick was as much astonished at this invitation as if he had really been invited by the Mayor to dine with him and the Board of Aldermen. Mr. Greyson was evidently a rich man, and yet he had actually invited two boot-blacks to dine with him.

"I guess we'd better go home, sir," said Dick, hesitating.

"I don't think you can have any very pressing engagements to interfere with your accepting my invitation," said Mr. Greyson, good-humoredly, for he understood the reasons of Dick's hesitation. "So I take it for granted that you both accept."

Before Dick fairly knew what he intended to do, he was walking down Fifth Avenue with his new friends.

Now, our young hero was not naturally bashful; but he certainly felt so now, especially as Miss Ida Greyson chose to walk by his side, leaving Henry Fosdick to walk with her father and mother.

"What is your name?" asked Ida, pleasantly.

Our hero was about to answer "Ragged Dick," when it occurred to him that in the present company he had better forget his old nickname.

"Dick Hunter," he answered.

"Dick!" repeated Ida. "That means Richard doesn't it?"

"Everybody calls me Dick."

"I have a cousin Dick," said the young lady, sociably. "His name is Dick Wilson. I suppose you don't know him?"

"No," said Dick.

"I like the name of Dick," said the young lady, with charming frankness.

Without being able to tell why, Dick felt rather glad she did. He plucked up courage to ask her name.

"My name is Ida," answered the young lady. "Do you like it?"

"Yes," said Dick. "It's a bully name."

Dick turned red as soon as he had said it, for he felt that he had not used the right expression.

The little girl broke into a silvery laugh.

"What a funny boy you are!" she said.

"I didn't mean it," said Dick, stammering. "I meant it's a tip-top name."

Here Ida laughed again, and Dick wished himself back in Mott Street.

"How old are you?" inquired Ida, continuing her examination.

"I'm fourteen,—goin' on fifteen," said Dick.

"You're a big boy of your age," said Ida. "My cousin Dick is a year older than you, but he isn't as large."

Dick looked pleased. Boys generally like to be told that they are large of their age.

"How old be you?" asked Dick, beginning to feel more at his ease.

"I'm nine years old," said Ida. "I go to Miss Jarvis's school. I've just begun to learn French. Do you know French?"

"Not enough to hurt me," said Dick.

Ida laughed again, and told him that he was a droll boy.

"Do you like it?" asked Dick.

"I like it pretty well, except the verbs. I can't remember them well. Do you go to school?"

"I'm studying with a private tutor," said Dick.

"Are you? So is my cousin Dick. He's going to college this year. Are you going to college?"

"Not this year."

"Because, if you did, you know you'd be in the same class with my cousin. It would be funny to have two Dicks in one class."

They turned down Twenty-fourth Street, passing the Fifth Avenue Hotel on the left, and stopped before an elegant house with a brown stone front. The bell was rung, and the door being opened, the boys, somewhat abashed, followed Mr. Greyson into a handsome hall. They were told where to hang their hats, and a moment afterwards were ushered into a comfortable dining-room, where a table was spread for dinner.

Dick took his seat on the edge of a sofa, and was tempted to rub his eyes to make sure that he was really awake. He could hardly believe that he was a guest in so fine a mansion.

Ida helped to put the boys at their ease.

"Do you like pictures?" she asked.

"Very much," answered Henry.

The little girl brought a book of handsome engravings, and, seating herself beside Dick, to whom she seemed to have taken a decided fancy, commenced showing them to him.

"There are the Pyramids of Egypt," she said, pointing to one engraving.

"What are they for?" asked Dick, puzzled. "I don't see any winders."

"No," said Ida, "I don't believe anybody lives there. Do they, papa?"

"No, my dear. They are used for the burial of the dead. The largest of them is said to be the loftiest building in the world with one exception. The spire of the Cathedral of Strasburg is twenty-four feet higher, if I remember rightly."

"Is Egypt near here?" asked Dick.

"Oh, no, it's ever so many miles off; about four or five hundred. Didn't you know?"

"No," said Dick. "I never heard."

"You don't appear to be very accurate in your information, Ida," said her mother. "Four or five thousand miles would be considerably nearer the truth."

After a little more conversation they sat down to dinner. Dick seated himself in an embarrassed way. He was very much afraid of doing or saying something which would be considered an impropriety, and had the uncomfortable feeling that everybody was looking at him, and watching his behavior.

"Where do you live, Dick?" asked Ida, familiarly.

"In Mott Street."

"Where is that?"

"More than a mile off."

"Is it a nice street?"

"Not very," said Dick. "Only poor folks live there."

"Are you poor?"

"Little girls should be seen and not heard," said her mother, gently.

"If you are," said Ida, "I'll give you the five-dollar gold-piece aunt gave me for a birthday present."

"Dick cannot be called poor, my child," said Mrs. Grey-son, "since he earns his living by his own exertions."

"Do you earn your living?" asked Ida, who was a very

inquisitive young lady, and not easily silenced. "What do you do?"

Dick blushed violently. At such a table, and in presence of the servant who was standing at that moment behind his chair, he did not like to say that he was a shoe-black, although he well knew that there was nothing dishonorable in the occupation.

Mr. Greyson perceived his feelings, and to spare them said, "You are too inquisitive, Ida. Some time Dick may tell you, but you know we don't talk of business on Sundays."

Dick in his embarrassment had swallowed a large spoonful of hot soup, which made him turn red in the face. For the second time, in spite of the prospect of the best dinner he had ever eaten, he wished himself back in Mott Street. Henry Fosdick was more easy and unembarrassed than Dick, not having led such a vagabond and neglected life. But it was to Dick that Ida chiefly directed her conversation, having apparently taken a fancy to his frank and handsome face. I believe I have already said that Dick was a very good-looking boy, especially now since he kept his face clean. He had a frank, honest expression, which generally won its way to the favor of those with whom he came in contact.

Dick got along pretty well at the table by dint of noticing how the rest acted, but there was one thing he could not manage, eating with his fork, which, by the way, he thought a very singular arrangement.

At length they arose from the table, somewhat to Dick's relief. Again Ida devoted herself to the boys, and exhibited a profusely illustrated Bible for their entertainment. Dick was interested in looking at the pictures, though he knew very little of their subjects. Henry Fosdick was much better informed; as might have been expected.

When the boys were about to leave the house with Mr. Greyson for the Sunday school, Ida placed her hand on Dick's, and said persuasively, "You'll come again, Dick, won't you?"

"Thank you," said Dick, "I'd like to," and he could not help thinking Ida the nicest girl he had ever seen.

"Yes," said Mrs. Greyson, hospitably, "we shall be glad to see you both here again."

"Thank you very much," said Henry Fosdick, gratefully. "We shall like very much to come."

I will not dwell upon the hour spent in Sunday school, nor upon the remarks of Mr. Greyson to his class. He found Dick's ignorance of religious subjects so great that he was obliged to begin at the beginning with him. Dick was interested in hearing the children sing, and readily promised to come again the next Sunday.

When the service was over Dick and Henry walked homewards. Dick could not help letting his thoughts rest on the sweet little girl who had given him so cordial a welcome, and hoping that he might meet her again.

"Mr. Greyson is a nice man,—isn't he, Dick?" asked Henry, as they were turning into Mott Street, and were already in sight of their lodging-house.

"Ain't he, though?" said Dick. "He treated us just as if we were young gentlemen."

"Ida seemed to take a great fancy to you."

"She's a tip-top girl," said Dick, "but she asked so many questions that I didn't know what to say."

He had scarcely finished speaking, when a stone whizzed by his head, and, turning quickly, he saw Micky Maguire running round the corner of the street which they had just passed.

CHAPTER XVIII

Micky Maguire's Second Defeat

DICK was no coward. Nor was he in the habit of submitting passively to an insult. When, therefore, he recognized Micky Maguire as his assailant, he instantly turned and gave chase. Micky anticipated pursuit, and ran at his utmost speed. It is doubtful if Dick would have overtaken him, but Micky had the ill luck to trip just as he had entered a narrow alley, and, falling with some violence, received a sharp blow from the hard stones, which made him scream with pain.

"Ow!" he whined. "Don't you hit a feller when he's down."

"What made you fire that stone at me?" demanded our hero, looking down at the fallen bully.

"Just for fun," said Micky.

"It would have been a very agreeable s'prise if it had hit me," said Dick. "S'posin' I fire a rock at you jest for fun."

"Don't!" exclaimed Micky, in alarm.

"It seems you don't like agreeable s'prises," said Dick, "any more'n the man did what got hooked by a cow one mornin', before breakfast. It didn't improve his appetite much."

"I've most broke my arm," said Micky, ruefully, rubbing the affected limb.

"If it's broke you can't fire no more stones, which is a very cheerin' reflection," said Dick. "Ef you haven't money enough to buy a wooden one I'll lend you a quarter. There's one good thing about wooden ones, they ain't liable to get cold in winter, which is another cheerin' reflection."

"I don't want none of yer cheerin' reflections," said Micky, sullenly. "Yer company ain't wanted here."

"Thank you for your polite invitation to leave," said Dick, bowing ceremoniously. "I'm willin' to go, but ef you throw any more stones at me, Micky Maguire, I'll hurt you worse than the stones did."

The only answer made to this warning was a scowl from his fallen opponent. It was quite evident that Dick had the best of it, and he thought it prudent to say nothing.

"As I've got a friend waitin' outside, I shall have to tear myself away," said Dick. "You'd better not throw any more stones, Micky Maguire, for it don't seem to agree with your constitution."

Micky muttered something which Dick did not stay to hear. He backed out of the alley, keeping watchful eye on his fallen foe, and rejoined Henry Fosdick, who was waiting his return.

"Who was it, Dick?" he asked.

"A partic'lar friend of mine, Micky Maguire," said Dick. "He playfully fired a rock at my head as a mark of his 'fection. He loves me like a brother, Micky does."

"Rather a dangerous kind of a friend, I should think," said Fosdick. "He might have killed you."

"I've warned him not to be so 'fectionate another time," said Dick.

"I know him," said Henry Fosdick. "He's at the head of a gang of boys living at the Five-Points. He threatened to whip me once because a gentleman employed me to black his boots instead of him."

"He's been at the Island two or three times for stealing," said Dick. "I guess he won't touch me again. He'd rather get hold of small boys. If he ever does anything to you, Fosdick, just let me know, and I'll give him a thrashing."

Dick was right. Micky Maguire was a bully, and like most bullies did not fancy tackling boys whose strength was equal or superior to his own. Although he hated Dick more than ever, because he thought our hero was putting on airs, he had too lively a remembrance of his strength and courage to venture upon another open attack. He contented himself, therefore, whenever he met Dick, with scowling at him. Dick took this very philosophically, remarking that, "if it was soothin' to Micky's feelings, he might go ahead, as it didn't hurt him much."

It will not be necessary to chronicle the events of the next few weeks. A new life had commenced for Dick. He no longer haunted the gallery of the Old Bowery; and even Tony Pastor's hospitable doors had lost their old attractions. He spent two hours every evening in study. His progress was astonishingly rapid. He was gifted with a natural quickness; and he was stimulated by the desire to acquire a fair education as a means of "growin' up 'spectable," as he termed it. Much was due also to the patience and perseverance of Henry Fosdick, who made a capital teacher.

"You're improving wonderfully, Dick," said his friend, one evening, when Dick had read an entire paragraph without a mistake.

"Am I?" said Dick, with satisfaction.

"Yes. If you'll buy a writing-book to-morrow, we can begin writing to-morrow evening."

"What else do you know, Henry?" asked Dick.

"Arithmetic, and geography, and grammar."

"What a lot you know!" said Dick, admiringly.

"I don't *know* any of them," said Fosdick. "I've only studied them. I wish I knew a great deal more."

"I'll be satisfied when I know as much as you," said Dick.

"It seems a great deal to you now, Dick, but in a few months you'll think differently. The more you know, the more you'll want to know."

"Then there ain't any end to learnin'?" said Dick.

"No."

"Well," said Dick, "I guess I'll be as much as sixty before I know everything."

"Yes; as old as that, probably," said Fosdick, laughing.

"Anyway, you know too much to be blackin' boots. Leave that to ignorant chaps like me."

"You won't be ignorant long, Dick."

"You'd ought to get into some office or countin'-room."

"I wish I could," said Fosdick, earnestly. "I don't succeed very well at blacking boots. You make a great deal more than I do."

"That's cause I ain't troubled with bashfulness," said Dick. "Bashfulness ain't as natural to me as it is to you. I'm always on hand, as the cat said to the milk. You'd better give up shines, Fosdick, and give your 'tention to mercantile pursuits."

"I've thought of trying to get a place," said Fosdick; "but no one would take me with these clothes"; and he directed his glance to his well-worn suit, which he kept as neat as he could, but which, in spite of all his care, began to show decided marks of use. There was also here and there a stain of blacking upon it, which, though an advertisement of his profession, scarcely added to its good appearance.

"I almost wanted to stay at home from Sunday school last Sunday," he continued, "because I thought everybody would notice how dirty and worn my clothes had got to be."

"If my clothes wasn't two sizes too big for you," said

Dick, generously, "I'd change. You'd look as if you'd got into your great-uncle's suit by mistake."

"You're very kind, Dick, to think of changing," said Fosdick, "for your suit is much better than mine; but I don't think that mine would suit you very well. The pants would show a little more of your ankles than is the fashion, and you couldn't eat a very hearty dinner without bursting the buttons off the vest."

"That wouldn't be very convenient," said Dick. "I ain't fond of lacin' to show my elegant figger. But I say," he added with a sudden thought, "how much money have we got in the savings bank?"

Fosdick took a key from his pocket, and went to the drawer in which the bank-books were kept, and, opening it, brought them out for inspection.

It was found that Dick had the sum of eighteen dollars and ninety cents placed to his credit, while Fosdick had six dollars and forty-five cents. To explain the large difference, it must be remembered that Dick had deposited five dollars before Henry deposited anything, being the amount he had received as a gift from Mr. Whitney.

"How much does that make, the lot of it?" asked Dick. "I ain't much on figgers yet, you know."

"It makes twenty-five dollars and thirty-five cents, Dick," said his companion, who did not understand the thought which suggested the question.

"Take it, and buy some clothes, Henry," said Dick, shortly.

"What, your money too?"

"In course."

"No, Dick, you are too generous. I couldn't think of it. Almost three-quarters of the money is yours. You must spend it on yourself."

"I don't need it," said Dick.

"You may not need it now, but you will some time."

"I shall have some more then."

"That may be; but it wouldn't be fair for me to use your money, Dick. I thank you all the same for your kindness."

"Well, I'll lend it to you, then," persisted Dick, "and you can pay me when you get to be a rich merchant."

"But it isn't likely I ever shall be one."

"How d'you know? I went to a fortun' teller once, and she told me I was born under a lucky star with a hard name, and I should have a rich man for my particular friend, who would make my fortun'. I guess you are going to be the rich man."

Fosdick laughed, and steadily refused for some time to avail himself of Dick's generous proposal; but at length, perceiving that our hero seemed much disappointed, and would be really glad if his offer were accepted, he agreed to use as much as might be needful.

This at once brought back Dick's good-humor, and he entered with great enthusiasm into his friend's plans.

The next day they withdrew the money from the bank, and, when business got a little slack, in the afternoon, set out in search of a clothing store. Dick knew enough of the city to be able to find a place where a good bargain could be obtained. He was determined that Fosdick should have a good serviceable suit, even if it took all the money they had. The result of their search was that for twenty-three dollars Fosdick obtained a very neat outfit, including a couple of shirts, a hat, and a pair of shoes, besides a dark mixed suit, which appeared stout and of good quality.

"Shall I send the bundle home?" asked the salesman, impressed by the off-hand manner in which Dick drew out the money in payment for the clothes.

"Thank you," said Dick, "you're very kind, but I'll take it home myself, and you can allow me something for my trouble."

"All right," said the clerk, laughing; "I'll allow it on your next purchase."

Proceeding to their apartment in Mott Street, Fosdick at

once tried on his new suit, and it was found to be an excellent fit. Dick surveyed his new friend with much satisfaction.

"You look like a young gentleman of fortun'," he said, "and do credit to your governor."

"I suppose that means you, Dick," said Fosdick, laughing.

"In course it does."

"You should say *of* course," said Fosdick, who, in virtue of his position as Dick's tutor, ventured to correct his language from time to time.

"How dare you correct your gov'nor?" said Dick, with comic indignation. "'I'll cut you off with a shillin', you young dog,' as the Markis says to his nephew in the play at the Old Bowery."

CHAPTER XIX

Fosdick Changes
His Business

Fosdick did not venture to wear his new clothes while engaged in his business. This he felt would have been wasteful extravagance. About ten o'clock in the morning, when business slackened, he went home, and dressing himself went to a hotel where he could see copies of the *Morning Herald* and *Sun,* and, noting down the places where a boy was wanted, went on a round of applications. But he found it no easy thing to obtain a place. Swarms of boys seemed to be out of employment, and it was not unusual to find from fifty to a hundred applicants for a single place.

There was another difficulty. It was generally desired that the boy wanted should reside with his parents. When Fosdick, on being questioned, revealed the fact of his having no parents, and being a boy of the street, this was generally sufficient of itself to insure a refusal. Merchants were afraid to trust one who had led such a vagabond life. Dick, who was always ready for an emergency, suggested borrowing a white wig, and passing himself off for Fosdick's father or grandfather. But Henry thought this might be rather a difficult character for our hero to sustain. After fifty applications and as many failures, Fosdick began to get discouraged. There seemed to be no way out of his present business, for which he felt unfitted.

"I don't know but I shall have to black boots all my life," he said, one day, despondently, to Dick.

"Keep a stiff upper lip," said Dick. "By the time you get to be a gray-headed veteran, you may get a chance to run errands for some big firm on the Bowery, which is a very cheerin' reflection."

So Dick by his drollery and perpetual good spirits kept up Fosdick's courage.

"As for me," said Dick, "I expect by that time to lay up a colossal fortun' out of shines, but live in princely style on the Avenoo."

But one morning, Fosdick, straying into French's Hotel, discovered the following advertisement in the columns of "The Herald,"—

"WANTED—A smart, capable boy to run errands, and make himself generally useful in a hat and cap store. Salary three dollars a week at first. Inquire at No.— Broadway, after ten o'clock, A.M."

He determined to make application, and, as the City Hall clock just then struck the hour indicated, lost no time in proceeding to the store, which was only a few blocks distant from the Astor House. It was easy to find the store, as from a dozen to twenty boys were already assembled in front of it. They surveyed each other askance, feeling that they were rivals, and mentally calculating each other's chances.

"There isn't much chance for me," said Fosdick to Dick, who had accompanied him. "Look at all these boys. Most of them have good homes, I suppose, and good recommendations, while I have nobody to refer to."

"Go ahead," said Dick. "Your chance is as good as anybody's."

While this was passing between Dick and his companion, one of the boys, a rather supercilious-looking young gentleman, genteelly dressed, and evidently having a very high opinion of his dress and himself, turned suddenly to Dick, and remarked,—

"I've seen you before."

"Oh, have you?" said Dick, whirling round; "then p'r'aps you'd like to see me behind."

At this unexpected answer all the boys burst into a laugh with the exception of the questioner, who evidently considered that Dick had been disrespectful.

"I've seen you somewhere," he said, in a surly tone, correcting himself.

"Most likely you have," said Dick. "That's where I generally keep myself."

There was another laugh at the expense of Roswell Crawford, for that was the name of the young aristocrat. But he had his revenge ready. No boy relishes being an object of ridicule, and it was with a feeling of satisfaction that he retorted,—

"I know you for all your impudence. You're nothing but a boot-black."

This information took the boys who were standing around by surprise, for Dick was well-dressed, and had none of the implements of his profession with him.

"S'pose I be," said Dick. "Have you got any objection?"

"Not at all," said Roswell, curling his lip; "only you'd better stick to blacking boots, and not try to get into a store."

"Thank you for your kind advice," said Dick. "Is it gratooitous, or do you expect to be paid for it?"

"You're an impudent fellow."

"That's a very cheerin' reflection," said Dick, good-naturedly.

"Do you expect to get this place when there's gentlemen's sons applying for it? A boot-black in a store! That would be a good joke."

Boys as well as men are selfish, and, looking upon Dick as a possible rival, the boys who listened seemed disposed to take the same view of the situation.

"That's what I say," said one of them, taking sides with Roswell.

"Don't trouble yourselves," said Dick. "I ain't a-goin' to cut you out. I can't afford to give up a independent and loocrative profession for a salary of three dollars a week."

"Hear him talk!" said Roswell Crawford, with an unpleasant sneer. "If you are not trying to get the place, what are you here for?"

"I came with a friend of mine," said Dick, indicating Fosdick, "who's goin' in for the situation."

"Is he a boot-black, too?" demanded Roswell, superciliously.

"He!" retorted Dick, loftily. "Didn't you know his father was a member of Congress, and intimately acquainted with all the biggest men in the State?"

The boys surveyed Fosdick as if they did not quite know whether to credit this statement, which, for the credit of Dick's veracity, it will be observed he did not assert, but only propounded in the form of a question. There was no time for comment, however, as just then the proprietor of the store came to the door, and, casting his eyes over the waiting group, singled out Roswell Crawford, and asked him to enter.

"Well, my lad, how old are you?"

"Fourteen years old," said Roswell, consequentially.

"Are your parents living?"

"Only my mother. My father is dead. He was a gentleman," he added complacently.

"Oh, was he?" said the shop-keeper. "Do you live in the city?"

"Yes, sir. In Clinton Place."

"Have you ever been in a situation before?"

"Yes, sir," said Roswell, a little reluctantly.

"Where was it?"

"In an office on Dey Street."

"How long were you there?"

"A week."

"It seems to me that was a short time. Why did you not stay longer?"

"Because," said Rosewell, loftily, "the man wanted me to get to the office at eight o'clock, and make the fire. I'm a gentleman's son, and am not used to such dirty work."

"Indeed!" said the shop-keeper. "Well, young gentleman, you may step aside a few minutes. I will speak with some of the other boys before making my selection."

Several other boys were called in and questioned. Roswell stood by and listened with an air of complacency. He could not help thinking his chances the best. "The man can see I'm a gentleman, and will do credit to his store," he thought.

At length it came to Fosdick's turn. He entered with no very sanguine anticipations of success. Unlike Roswell, he set a very low estimate upon his qualifications when compared with those of other applicants. But his modest bearing, and quiet, gentlemanly manner, entirely free from pretension, prepossessed the shop-keeper, who was a sensible man, in his favor.

"Do you reside in the city?" he asked.

"Yes, sir," said Henry.

"What is your age?"

"Twelve."

"Have you ever been in any situation?"

"No, sir."

"I should like to see a specimen of your handwriting. Here, take the pen and write your name."

Henry Fosdick had a very handsome handwriting for a boy of his age, while Roswell, who had submitted to the same test, could do little more than scrawl.

"Do you reside with your parents?"

"No, sir, they are dead."

"Where do you live, then?"

"In Mott Street."

Roswell curled his lip when this name was pronounced, for Mott Street, as my New York readers know, is in the immediate neighborhood of the Five-Points, and very far from a fashionable locality.

"Have you any testimonials to present?" asked Mr. Henderson, for that was his name.

Fosdick hesitated. This was the question which he had foreseen would give him trouble.

But at this moment it happened most opportunely that Mr. Greyson entered the shop with the intention of buying a hat.

"Yes," said Fosdick, promptly; "I will refer to this gentleman."

"How do you do, Fosdick?" asked Mr. Greyson, noticing him for the first time. "How do you happen to be here?"

"I am applying for a place, sir," said Fosdick. "May I refer the gentleman to you?"

"Certainly, I shall be glad to speak a good word for you. Mr. Henderson, this is a member of my Sunday school class, for whose good qualities and good abilities I can speak confidently."

"That will be sufficient," said the shop-keeper, who knew Mr. Greyson's high character and position. "He could have no better recommendation. You may come to the store tomorrow morning at half-past seven o'clock. The pay will be three dollars a week for the first six months. If I am satisfied with you, I shall then raise it to five dollars."

The other boys looked disappointed, but none more so

than Roswell Crawford. He would have cared less if any one else had obtained the situation; but for a boy who lived in Mott Street to be preferred to him, a gentleman's son, he considered indeed humiliating. In a spirit of petty spite, he was tempted to say, "He's a boot-black. Ask him if he isn't."

"He's an honest and intelligent lad," said Mr. Greyson. "As for you, young man, I only hope you have one-half his good qualities."

Roswell Crawford left the store in disgust, and the other unsuccessful applicants with him.

"What luck, Fosdick?" asked Dick, eagerly, as his friend came out of the store.

"I've got the place," said Fosdick, in accents of satisfaction; "but it was only because Mr. Greyson spoke up for me."

"He's a trump," said Dick, enthusiastically.

The gentleman, so denominated, came out before the boys went away, and spoke with them kindly.

Both Dick and Henry were highly pleased at the success of the application. The pay would indeed be small, but, expended economically, Fosdick thought he could get along on it, receiving his room rent, as before, in return for his services as Dick's private tutor. Dick determined, as soon as his education would permit, to follow his companion's example.

"I don't know as you'll be willin' to room with a boot-black," he said to Henry, "now you're goin' into business."

"I couldn't room with a better friend, Dick," said Fosdick, affectionately, throwing his arm round our hero. "When we part, it'll be because you wish it."

So Fosdick entered upon a new career.

CHAPTER XX

Nine Months Later

THE next morning Fosdick rose early, put on his new suit, and, after getting breakfast, set out for the Broadway store in which he had obtained a position. He left his little blacking-box in the room.

"It'll do to brush my own shoes," he said. "Who knows but I may have to come back to it again?"

"No danger," said Dick; "I'll take care of the feet, and you'll have to look after the heads, now you're in a hat-store."

"I wish you had a place too," said Fosdick.

"I don't know enough yet," said Dick. "Wait till I've grad-ooated."

"And can put A. B. after your name."

"What's that?"

"It stands for Bachelor of Arts. It's a degree that students get when they graduate from college."

"Oh," said Dick, "I didn't know but it meant A Boot-black. I can put that after my name now. Wouldn't Dick Hunter, A. B., sound tip-top?"

"I must be going," said Fosdick. "It won't do for me to be late the very first morning."

"That's the difference between you and me," said Dick. "I'm my own boss, and there ain't no one to find fault with me if I'm late. But I might as well be goin' too. There's a gent as comes down to his store pretty early that generally wants a shine."

The two boys parted at the Park. Fosdick crossed it, and proceeded to the hat-store, while Dick, hitching up his pants, began to look about him for a customer. It was seldom that Dick had to wait long. He was always on the alert, and if there was any business to do he was always sure to get his share of it. He had now a stronger inducement than ever to attend strictly to business; his little stock of money in the savings bank having been nearly exhausted by his liberality to his room-mate. He determined to be as economical as possible, and moreover to study as hard as he could, that he might be able to follow Fosdick's example, and obtain a place in a store or counting-room. As there were no striking incidents occurring in our hero's history within the next nine months, I propose to pass over that period, and recount the progress he made in that time.

Fosdick was still at the hat-store, having succeeded in giving perfect satisfaction to Mr. Henderson. His wages had just been raised to five dollars a week. He and Dick still kept house together at Mrs. Mooney's lodging-house, and lived very frugally, so that both were able to save up money. Dick had been unusually successful in business. He had several regular patrons, who had been drawn to him by his ready wit, and quick humor, and from two of them he had received presents of clothing, which had saved him any expense on that score. His income had averaged quite seven dollars a week in addition to this. Of this amount he was now obliged to pay one dollar weekly for the room which he and Fosdick occupied, but he was still able to save one half the remainder. At the end of nine months therefore, or thirty-nine weeks, it will be seen that he had accumulated no less a sum than one hundred and seventeen dollars. Dick may be excused for feeling like a capitalist when he looked at the long row of deposits in his little bank-book. There were other boys in the same business who had earned as much money, but they had had little care for the future, and spent as they went along, so that few could boast a bank-account, however small.

"You'll be a rich man some time, Dick," said Henry Fosdick, one evening.

"And live on Fifth Avenoo," said Dick.

"Perhaps so. Stranger things have happened."

"Well," said Dick, "if such a misfortin' should come upon me I should bear it like a man. When you see a Fifth Avenoo manshun for sale for a hundred and seventeen dollars, just let me know and I'll buy it as an investment."

"Two hundred and fifty years ago you might have bought one for that price, probably. Real estate wasn't very high among the Indians."

"Just my luck," said Dick; "I was born too late. I'd orter have been an Indian, and lived in splendor on my present capital."

"I'm afraid you'd have found your present business rather unprofitable at that time."

But Dick had gained something more valuable than money. He had studied regularly every evening, and his improvement had been marvellous. He could now read well, write a fair hand, and had studied arithmetic as far as Interest. Besides this he had obtained some knowledge of grammar and geography. If some of my boy readers, who have been studying for years, and got no farther than this, should think it incredible that Dick, in less than a year, and studying evenings only, should have accomplished it, they must remember that our hero was very much in earnest in his desire to improve. He knew that, in order to grow up respectable, he must be well advanced, and he was willing to work. But then the reader must not forget that Dick was naturally a smart boy. His street education had sharpened his faculties, and taught him to rely upon himself. He knew that it would take him a long time to reach the goal which he had set before him, and he had patience to keep on trying. He knew that he had only himself to depend upon, and he determined to make the most of himself,—a resolution which is the secret of success in nine cases out of ten.

"Dick," said Fosdick, one evening, after they had completed their studies, "I think you'll have to get another teacher soon."

"Why?" asked Dick, in some surprise. "Have you been offered a more loocrative position?"

"No," said Fosdick, "but I find I have taught you all I know myself. You are now as good a scholar as I am."

"Is that true?" said Dick, eagerly, a flush of gratification coloring his brown cheek.

"Yes," said Fosdick. "You've made wonderful progress. I propose, now that evening schools have begun, that we join one, and study together through the winter."

"All right," said Dick. "I'd be willin' to go now; but when I first began to study I was ashamed to have anybody know that I was so ignorant. Do you really mean, Fosdick, that I know as much as you?"

"Yes, Dick, it's true."

"Then I've got you to thank for it," said Dick, earnestly. "You've made me what I am."

"And haven't you paid me, Dick?"

"By payin' the room rent," said Dick, impulsively. "What's that? It isn't half enough. I wish you'd take half my money; you deserve it."

"Thank you, Dick, but you're too generous. You've more than paid me. Who was it took my part when all the other boys imposed upon me? And who gave me money to buy clothes, and so got me my situation?"

"Oh, that's nothing!" said Dick.

"It's a great deal, Dick. I shall never forget it. But now it seems to me you might try to get a situation yourself."

"Do I know enough?"

"You know as much as I do."

"Then I'll try," said Dick, decidedly.

"I wish there was a place in our store," said Fosdick. "It would be pleasant for us to be together."

"Never mind," said Dick; "there'll be plenty of other chances. P'r'aps A. T. Stewart might like a partner. I wouldn't ask more'n a quarter of the profits."

"Which would be a very liberal proposal on your part," said Fosdick, smiling. "But perhaps Mr. Stewart might object to a partner living on Mott Street."

"I'd just as lieves move to Fifth Avenoo," said Dick. "I ain't got no prejudices in favor of Mott Street."

"Nor I," said Fosdick, "and in fact I have been thinking it might be a good plan for us to move as soon as we could afford. Mrs. Mooney doesn't keep the room quite so neat as she might."

"No," said Dick." She ain't got no prejudices against dirt. Look at that towel."

Dick held up the article indicated, which had now seen service nearly a week, and hard service at that,—Dick's avocation causing him to be rather hard on towels.

"Yes," said Fosdick, "I've got about tired of it. I guess we can find some better place without having to pay much more. When we move, you must let me pay my share of the rent."

"We'll see about that," said Dick. "Do you propose to move to Fifth Avenoo?"

"Not just at present, but to some more agreeable neighborhood than this. We'll wait till you get a situation, and then we can decide."

A few days later, as Dick was looking about for customers in the neighborhood of the Park, his attention was drawn to a fellow boot-black, a boy about a year younger than himself, who appeared to have been crying.

"What's the matter, Tom?" asked Dick. "Haven't you had luck to-day?"

"Pretty good," said the boy; "but we're havin' hard times at home. Mother fell last week and broke her arm, and to-morrow we've got to pay the rent, and if we don't the landlord says he'll turn us out."

"Haven't you got anything except what you earn?" asked Dick.

"No," said Tom, "not now. Mother used to earn three or four dollars a week; but she can't do nothin' now, and my little sister and brother are too young."

Dick had quick sympathies. He had been so poor himself, and obliged to submit to so many privations that he knew from personal experience how hard it was. Tom Wilkins he knew as an excellent boy who never squandered his money, but faithfully carried it home to his mother. In the days of his own extravagance and shiftlessness he had once or twice asked Tom to accompany him to the Old Bowery or Tony Pastor's, but Tom had always steadily refused.

"I am sorry for you, Tom," he said. "How much do you owe for rent?"

"Two weeks now," said Tom.

"How much is it a week?"

"Two dollars a week—that makes four."

"Have you got anything towards it?"

"No; I've had to spend all my money for food for mother and the rest of us. I've had pretty hard work to do that. I don't know what we'll do. I haven't any place to go to, and I'm afraid mother'll get cold in her arm."

"Can't you borrow the money somewhere?" asked Dick.

Tom shook his head despondingly.

"All the people I know are as poor as I am," said he.

"They'd help me if they could, but it's hard work for them to get along themselves."

"I'll tell you what, Tom," said Dick, impulsively, "I'll stand your friend."

"Have you got any money?" asked Tom, doubtfully.

"Got any money!" repeated Dick. "Don't you know that I run a bank on my own account? How much is it you need?"

"Four dollars," said Tom. "If we don't pay that before to-morrow night, out we go. You haven't got as much as that, have you?"

"Here are three dollars," said Dick, drawing out his pocket-book. "I'll let you have the rest to-morrow, and maybe a little more."

"You're a right down good fellow, Dick," said Tom; "but won't you want it yourself?"

"Oh, I've got some more," said Dick.

"Maybe I'll never be able to pay you."

"'Spose you don't," said Dick; "I guess I won't fail."

"I won't forget it, Dick. I hope I'll be able to do somethin' for you sometime."

"All right," said Dick. "I'd ought to help you. I haven't got no mother to look out for. I wish I had."

There was a tinge of sadness in his tone, as he pronounced the last four words; but Dick's temperament was sanguine, and he never gave way to unavailing sadness. Accordingly he began to whistle as he turned away, only adding, "I'll see you to-morrow, Tom."

The three dollars which Dick had handed to Tom Wilkins were his savings for the present week. It was now Thursday afternoon. His rent, which amounted to a dollar, he expected to save out of the earnings of Friday and Saturday. In order to give Tom the additional assistance he had promised, Dick would be obliged to have recourse to his bank-savings. He

would not have ventured to trench upon it for any other reason but this. But he felt that it would be selfish to allow Tom
and his mother to suffer when he had it in his power to re-
lieve them. But Dick was destined to be surprised, and that
in a disagreeable manner, when he reached home.

CHAPTER XXI

Dick Loses His Bank-book

IT was hinted at the close of the last chapter that Dick was destined to be disagreeably surprised on reaching home.

Having agreed to give further assistance to Tom Wilkins, he was naturally led to go to the drawer where he and Fosdick kept their bank-books. To his surprise and uneasiness *the drawer proved to be empty.*

"Come here a minute, Fosdick," he said.

"What's the matter, Dick?"

"I can't find my bank-book, nor yours either. What's 'come of them?"

"I took mine with me this morning, thinking I might want to put in a little more money. I've got it in my pocket, now."

"But where's mine?" asked Dick, perplexed.

"I don't know. I saw it in the drawer when I took mine this morning."

"Are you sure?"

"Yes, positive, for I looked into it to see how much you had got."

"Did you lock it again?" asked Dick.

"Yes; didn't you have to unlock it just now?"

"So I did," said Dick. "But it's gone now. Somebody opened it with a key that fitted the lock, and then locked it ag'in."

"That must have been the way."

"It's rather hard on a feller," said Dick, who, for the first time since we became acquainted with him, began to feel down-hearted.

"Don't give it up, Dick. You haven't lost the money, only the bank-book."

"Ain't that the same thing?"

"No. You can go to the bank to-morrow morning, as soon as it opens, and tell them you have lost the book, and ask them not to pay the money to any one except yourself."

"So I can," said Dick, brightening up. "That is, if the thief hasn't been to the bank to-day."

"If he has, they might detect him by his handwriting."

"I'd like to get ahold of the one that stole it," said Dick, indignantly. "I'd give him a good lickin'."

"It must have been somebody in the house. Suppose we go and see Mrs. Mooney. She may know whether anybody came into our room to-day."

The two boys went downstairs, and knocked at the door of a little back sitting-room where Mrs. Mooney generally spent her evenings. It was a shabby little room, with a threadbare carpet on the floor, the walls covered with a certain large-figured paper, patches of which had been stripped off here and there, exposing the plaster, the remainder being defaced by dirt and grease. But Mrs. Mooney had one of those comfortable temperaments which are tolerant of dirt, and didn't mind it in the least. She was seated beside a small pine work-table, industriously engaged in mending stockings.

"Good-evening, Mrs. Mooney," said Fosdick, politely.

"Good-evening," said the landlady. "Sit down, if you can find chairs. I'm hard at work as you see, but a poor lone widder can't afford to be idle."

"We can't stop long, Mrs. Mooney, but my friend here has had something taken from his room to-day, and we thought we'd come and see you about it."

"What is it?" asked the landlady. "You don't think I'd take anything? If I am poor, it's an honest name I've always had, as all my lodgers can testify."

"Certainly not, Mrs. Mooney; but there are others in the house that may not be honest. My friend has lost his bankbook. It was safe in the drawer this morning, but to-night it is not to be found."

"How much money was there in it?" asked Mrs. Mooney.

"Over a hundred dollars," said Fosdick.

"It was my whole fortun'," said Dick. "I was goin' to buy a house next year."

Mrs. Mooney was evidently surprised to learn the extent of Dick's wealth, and was disposed to regard him with increased respect.

"Was the drawer locked?" she asked.

"Yes."

"Then it couldn't have been Bridget. I don't think she has any keys."

"She wouldn't know what a bank-book was," said Fosdick. "You didn't see any of the lodgers go into our room to-day, did you?"

"I shouldn't wonder if it was Jim Travis," said Mrs. Mooney, suddenly.

This James Travis was a bar-tender in a low groggery in Mulberry Street, and had been for a few weeks an inmate of Mrs. Mooney's lodging-house. He was a coarse-looking fellow who, from his appearance, evidently patronized liberally the liquor he dealt out to others. He occupied a room opposite Dick's, and was often heard by the two boys reeling upstairs in a state of intoxication, uttering shocking oaths.

This Travis had made several friendly overtures to Dick and his room-mate, and had invited them to call round at the bar-room where he tended, and take something. But this invitation had never been accepted, partly because the boys were better engaged in the evening, and partly because neither of them had taken a fancy to Mr. Travis; which certainly was not strange, for nature had not gifted him with many charms, either of personal appearance or manners. The rejection of his friendly proffers had caused him to take a dislike to Dick and Henry, whom he considered stiff and unsocial.

"What makes you think it was Travis?" asked Fosdick. "He isn't at home in the daytime."

"But he was to-day. He said he had got a bad cold, and had to come home for a clean handkerchief."

"Did you see him?" asked Dick.

"Yes," said Mrs. Mooney. "Bridget was hanging out clothes, and I went to the door to let him in."

"I wonder if he had a key that would fit our drawer," said Fosdick.

"Yes," said Mrs. Mooney. "The bureaus in the two rooms are just alike. I got 'em at auction, and most likely the locks is the same."

"It must have been he," said Dick, looking towards Fosdick.

"Yes," said Fosdick, "it looks like it."

"What's to be done? That's what I'd like to know," said Dick. "Of course he'll say he hasn't got it; and he won't be such a fool as to leave it in his room."

"If he hasn't been to the bank, it's all right," said Fosdick. "You can go there the first thing to-morrow morning, and stop their paying any money on it."

"But I can't get any money on it myself," said Dick. "I told Tom Wilkins I'd let him have some more money to-morrow, or his sick mother'll have to turn out of their lodgin's."

"How much money were you going to give him?"

"I gave him three dollars to-day, and was goin' to give him two dollars to-morrow."

"I've got the money, Dick. I didn't go to the bank this morning."

"All right. I'll take it, and pay you back next week."

"No, Dick; if you've given three dollars, you must let me give two."

"No, Fosdick, I'd rather give the whole. You know I've got more money than you. No, I haven't, either," said Dick, the memory of his loss flashing upon him. "I thought I was rich this morning, but now I'm in destitoot circumstances."

"Cheer up, Dick; you'll get your money back."

"I hope so," said our hero, rather ruefully.

The fact was that our friend Dick was beginning to feel what is so often experienced by men who do business of a more important character and on a larger scale than he, the bitterness of a reverse of circumstances. With one hundred dollars and over carefully laid away in the savings bank, he had felt quite independent. Wealth is comparative, and Dick probably felt as rich as many men who are worth a hundred thousand dollars. He was beginning to feel the advantages of his steady self-denial, and to experience the pleasures of property. Not that Dick was likely to be unduly attached to money. Let it be said to his credit that it had never given him so much satisfaction as when it enabled him to help Tom Wilkins in his trouble.

Besides this, there was another thought that troubled him. When he obtained a place he could not expect to receive as much as he was now making from blacking boots,—probably not more than three dollars a week,—while his expenses without clothing would amount to four dollars. To make up the deficiency he had confidently relied upon his savings, which would be sufficient to carry him along for a year, if necessary. If he should not recover his money, he would be compelled to continue a boot-black for at least six months longer; and this was rather a discouraging reflection. On the whole it is not to be wondered at that Dick felt unusually sober this evening, and that neither of the boys felt much like studying.

The two boys consulted as to whether it would be best to speak to Travis about it. It was not altogether easy to decide. Fosdick was opposed to it.

"It will only put him on his guard," said he, "and I don't see it will do any good. Of course he will deny it. We'd better keep quiet, and watch him, and, by giving notice at the bank, we can make sure that he doesn't get any money on it. If he does present himself at the bank, they will know at once that he is a thief, and he can be arrested."

This view seemed reasonable, and Dick resolved to adopt it. On the whole, he began to think prospects were brighter than he had at first supposed, and his spirits rose a little.

"How'd he know I had any bank-book? That's what I can't make out," he said.

"Don't you remember?" said Fosdick, after a moment's thought, "we were speaking of our savings, two or three evenings since?"

"Yes," said Dick.

"Our door was a little open at the time, and I heard somebody come upstairs, and stop a minute in front of it. It must have been Jim Travis. In that way he probably found out about your money, and took the opportunity to-day to get hold of it."

This might or might not be the correct explanation. At all events it seemed probable.

The boys were just on the point of going to bed, later in the evening, when a knock was heard at the door, and, to their no little surprise, their neighbor, Jim Travis, proved to be the caller. He was a sallow-complexioned young man, with dark hair and bloodshot eyes.

He darted a quick glance from one to the other as he entered, which did not escape the boys' notice.

"How are ye, to-night?" he said, sinking into one of the two chairs with which the room was scantily furnished.

"Jolly," said Dick. "How are you?"

"Tired as a dog," was the reply. "Hard work and poor pay; that's the way with me. I wanted to go to the theatre, to-night, but I was hard up, and couldn't raise the cash."

Here he darted another quick glance at the boys; but neither betrayed anything.

"You don't go out much, do you?" he said.

"Not much," said Fosdick. "We spend our evenings in study."

"That's precious slow," said Travis, rather contemptuously. "What's the use of studying so much? You don't expect to be a lawyer, do you, or anything of that sort?"

"Maybe," said Dick. "I haven't made up my mind yet. If my feller-citizens should want me to go to Congress some time, I shouldn't want to disapp'int 'em; and then readin' and writin' might come handy."

"Well," said Travis, rather abruptly, "I'm tired, and I guess I'll turn in."

"Good-night," said Fosdick.

The boys looked at each other as their visitor left the room.

"He came in to see if we'd missed the bank-book," said Dick.

"And to turn off suspicion from himself, by letting us know he had no money," added Fosdick.

"That's so," said Dick. "I'd like to have searched them pockets of his."

CHAPTER XXII

Tracking the Thief

FOSDICK was right in supposing that Jim Travis had stolen the bank-book. He was also right in supposing that that worthy young man had come to the knowledge of Dick's savings by what he had accidentally overheard. Now, Travis, like a very large number of young men of his class, was able to dispose of a larger amount of money than he was able to earn. Moreover, he had no great fancy for work at all, and would have been glad to find some other way of obtaining money enough to pay his expenses. He had recently received a letter from an old companion, who had strayed out to California, and going at once to the mines had been lucky enough to get possession of a very remunerative claim. He wrote to Travis that he had already realized two thousand dollars from it, and expected to make his fortune within six months.

Two thousand dollars! This seemed to Travis a very large sum, and quite dazzled his imagination. He was at once inflamed with the desire to go out to California and try his luck. In his present situation he only received thirty dollars a month, which was probably all that his services were worth, but went a very little way towards gratifying his expensive tastes. Accordingly he determined to take the next steamer to the land of gold, if he could possibly manage to get money enough to pay the passage.

The price of a steerage passage at that time was seventy-five dollars,—not a large sum, certainly,—but it might as well have been seventy-five hundred for any chance James Travis had of raising the amount at present. His available funds consisted of precisely two dollars and a quarter; of which sum, one dollar and a half was due to his washerwoman. This, however, would not have troubled Travis much, and he would conveniently have forgotten all about it; but, even leaving this debt unpaid, the sum at his command would not help him materially towards paying his passage money.

Travis applied for help to two or three of his companions; but they were all of that kind who never keep an account with savings banks, but carry all their spare cash about with them. One of these friends offered to lend him thirty-seven cents, and another a dollar; but neither of these offers seemed to encourage him much. He was about giving up his project in despair, when he learned, accidentally, as we have already said, the extent of Dick's savings.

One hundred and seventeen dollars! Why, that would not only pay his passage, but carry him up to the mines, after he had arrived in San Francisco. He could not help thinking it over, and the result of this thinking was that he determined to borrow it of Dick without leave. Knowing that neither of the boys were in their rooms in the daytime, he came back in the course of the morning, and, being admitted by Mrs. Mooney herself, said, by way of accounting for his presence, that he had a cold, and had come back for a handkerchief. The landlady suspected nothing, and, returning at once to her work in the kitchen, left the coast clear.

Travis at once entered Dick's room, and, as there seemed

to be no other place for depositing money, tried the bureau-drawers. They were all readily opened, except one, which proved to be locked. This he naturally concluded must contain the money, and going back to his own chamber for the key of the bureau, tried it on his return, and found to his satisfaction that it would fit. When he discovered the bank-book, his joy was mingled with disappointment. He had expected to find bank-bills instead. This would have saved all further trouble, and would have been immediately available. Obtaining money at the savings bank would involve fresh risk. Travis hesitated whether to take it or not; but finally decided that it would be worth the trouble and hazard.

He accordingly slipped the book into his pocket, locked the drawer again, and, forgetting all about the handkerchief for which he had come home, went downstairs, and into the street.

There would have been time to go to the savings bank that day, but Travis had already been absent from his place of business some time, and did not venture to take the additional time required. Besides, not being very much used to savings banks, never having had occasion to use them, he thought it would be more prudent to look over the rules and regulations, and see if he could not get some information as to the way he ought to proceed. So the day passed, and Dick's money was left in safety at the bank.

In the evening, it occurred to Travis that it might be well to find out whether Dick had discovered his loss. This reflection it was that induced the visit which is recorded at the close of the last chapter. The result was that he was misled by the boys' silence on the subject, and concluded that nothing had yet been discovered.

"Good!" thought Travis, with satisfaction. "If they don't find out for twenty-four hours, it'll be too late, then, and I shall be all right."

There being a possibility of the loss being discovered before the boys went out in the morning, Travis determined to see them at that time, and judge whether such was the case. He waited, therefore, until he heard the boys come out, and then opened his own door.

"Morning, gents," said he, sociably. "Going to business?"

"Yes," said Dick. "I'm afraid my clerks'll be lazy if I ain't on hand."

"Good joke!" said Travis. "If you pay good wages, I'd like to speak for a place."

"I pay all I get myself," said Dick. "How's business with you?"

"So so. Why don't you call round, some time?"

"All my evenin's is devoted to literatoor and science," said Dick. "Thank you all the same."

"Where do you hang out?" inquired Travis, in choice language, addressing Fosdick.

"At Henderson's hat and cap store, on Broadway."

"I'll look in upon you some time when I want a title," said Travis. "I suppose you sell cheaper to your friends."

"I'll be as reasonable as I can," said Fosdick, not very cordially; for he did not much fancy having it supposed by his employer that such a disreputable-looking person as Travis was a friend of his.

However, Travis had no idea of showing himself at the Broadway store, and only said this by way of making conversation, and encouraging the boys to be social.

"You haven't any of you gents seen a pearl-handled knife, have you?" he asked.

"No," said Fosdick; "have you lost one?"

"Yes," said Travis, with unblushing falsehood. "I left it on my bureau a day or two since. I've missed one or two other little matters. Bridget don't look to me any too honest. Likely she's got 'em."

"What are you goin' to do about it?" said Dick.

"I'll keep mum unless I lose something more, and then

I'll kick up a row, and haul her over the coals. Have you missed anything?"

"No," said Fosdick, answering for himself, as he could do without violating the truth.

There was a gleam of satisfaction in the eyes of Travis, as he heard this.

"They haven't found it out yet," he thought. "I'll bag the money to-day, and then they may whistle for it."

Having no further object to serve in accompanying the boys, he bade them good-morning, and turned down another street.

"He's mighty friendly all of a sudden," said Dick.

"Yes," said Fosdick; "it's very evident what it all means. He wants to find out whether you have discovered your loss or not."

"But he didn't find out."

"No; we've put him on the wrong track. He means to get his money to-day, no doubt."

"My money," suggested Dick.

"I accept the correction," said Fosdick. "Of course, Dick, you'll be on hand as soon as the bank opens."

"In course I shall. Jim Travis'll find he's walked into the wrong shop."

"The bank opens at ten o'clock, you know."

"I'll be there on time."

The two boys separated.

"Good luck, Dick," said Fosdick, as he parted from him. "It'll all come out right, I think."

"I hope 'twill," said Dick.

He had recovered from his temporary depression, and made up his mind that the money would be recovered. He had no idea of allowing himself to be outwitted by Jim Travis, and enjoyed already, in anticipation, the pleasure of defeating his rascality.

It wanted two hours and a half yet to ten o'clock, and this

time to Dick was too precious to be wasted. It was the time
of his greatest harvest. He accordingly repaired to his usual
place of business, succeeded in obtaining six customers,
which yielded him sixty cents. He then went to a restaurant,
and got some breakfast. It was now half-past nine, and Dick,
feeling that it wouldn't do to be late, left his box in charge of
Johnny Nolan, and made his way to the bank.

The officers had not yet arrived, and Dick lingered on the
outside, waiting till they should come. He was not without a
little uneasiness, fearing that Travis might be as prompt as
himself, and finding him there, might suspect something,
and so escape the snare. But, though looking cautiously up
and down the street, he could discover no traces of the supposed thief. In due time ten o'clock struck, and immediately
afterwards the doors of the bank were thrown open, and our
hero entered.

As Dick had been in the habit of making a weekly visit
for the last nine months, the cashier had come to know him
by sight.

"You're early, this morning, my lad," he said pleasantly.
"Have you got some more money to deposit? You'll be getting rich, soon."

"I don't know about that," said Dick. "My bank-book's
been stole."

"Stolen!" echoed the cashier. "That's unfortunate. Not so
bad as it might be, though. The thief can't collect the money."

"That's what I came to see about," said Dick. "I was
afraid he might have got it already."

"He hasn't been here yet. Even if he had, I remember
you, and should have detected him. When was it taken?"

"Yesterday," said Dick. "I missed it in the evenin' when I
got home."

"Have you any suspicion as to the person who took it?"
asked the cashier.

Dick thereupon told all he knew as to the general character and suspicious conduct of Jim Travis, and the cashier agreed with him that he was probably the thief. Dick also gave his reason for thinking that he would visit the bank that morning, to withdraw the funds.

"Very good," said the cashier. "We'll be ready for him. What is the number of your book?"

"No. 5,678," said Dick.

"Now give me a little description of this Travis whom you suspect."

Dick accordingly furnished a brief outline sketch of Travis, not particularly complimentary to the latter.

"That will answer. I think I shall know him," said the cashier. "You may depend upon it that he shall receive no money on your account."

"Thank you," said Dick.

Considerably relieved in mind, our hero turned towards the door, thinking that there would be nothing gained by his remaining longer, while he would of course lose time.

He had just reached the doors, which were of glass, when through them he perceived James Travis himself just crossing the street, and apparently coming towards the bank. It would not do, of course, for him to be seen.

"Here he is," he exclaimed, hurrying back. "Can't you hide me somewhere? I don't want to be seen."

The cashier understood at once how the land lay. He quickly opened a little door, and admitted Dick behind the counter.

"Stoop down," he said, "so as not to be seen." Dick had hardly done so when Jim Travis opened the outer door, and, looking about him in a little uncertainty, walked up to the cashier's desk.

CHAPTER XXIII

Travis Is Arrested

JIM TRAVIS advanced into the bank with a doubtful step, knowing well that he was on a dishonest errand, and heartily wishing that he were well out of it. After a little hesitation, he approached the paying-teller, and, exhibiting the bank-book, said, "I want to get my money out."

The bank-officer took the book, and, after looking at it a moment, said, "How much do you want?"

"The whole of it," said Travis.

"You can draw out any part of it, but to draw out the whole requires a week's notice."

"Then I'll take a hundred dollars."

"Are you the person to whom the book belongs?"

"Yes, sir," said Travis, without hesitation.

"Your name is—"

"Hunter."

The bank-clerk went to a large folio volume, containing the names of depositors, and began to turn over the leaves. While he was doing this, he managed to send out a young man connected with the bank for a policeman. Travis did not perceive this, or did not suspect that it had anything to do with himself. Not being used to savings banks, he supposed the delay only what was usual. After a search, which was only intended to gain time that a policeman might be summoned, the cashier came back, and, sliding out a piece of paper to Travis, said, "It will be necessary for you to write an order for the money."

Travis took a pen, which he found on the ledge outside, and wrote the order, signing his name "Dick Hunter," having observed that name on the outside of the book.

"Your name is Dick Hunter, then?" said the cashier, taking the paper, and looking at the thief over his spectacles.

"Yes," said Travis, promptly.

"But," continued the cashier, "I find Hunter's age is put down on the bank-book as fourteen. Surely you must be more than that."

Travis would gladly have declared that he was only fourteen; but, being in reality twenty-three, and possessing a luxuriant pair of whiskers, this was not to be thought of. He began to feel uneasy.

"Dick Hunter's my younger brother," he said. "I'm getting out the money for him."

"I thought you said your own name was Dick Hunter," said the cashier.

"I said my name was Hunter," said Travis, ingeniously. "I didn't understand you."

"But you've signed the name of Dick Hunter to this order. How is that?" questioned the troublesome cashier.

Travis saw that he was getting himself into a tight place; but his self-possession did not desert him.

"I thought I must give my brother's name," he answered.

"What is your own name?"

"Henry Hunter."

"Can you bring any one to testify that the statement you are making is correct?"

"Yes, a dozen if you like," said Travis, boldly. "Give me the book, and I'll come back this afternoon. I didn't think there'd be such a fuss about getting out a little money."

"Wait a moment. Why don't your brother come himself?"

"Because he's sick. He's down with the measles," said Travis.

Here the cashier signed to Dick to rise and show himself. Our hero accordingly did so.

"You will be glad to find that he has recovered," said the cashier, pointing to Dick.

With an exclamation of anger and dismay, Travis, who saw the game was up, started for the door, feeling that safety made such a course prudent. But he was too late. He found himself confronted by a burly policeman, who seized him by the arm, saying, "Not so fast, my man. I want you."

"Let me go," exclaimed Travis, struggling to free himself.

"I'm sorry I can't oblige you," said the officer. "You'd better not make a fuss, or I may have to hurt you a little."

Travis sullenly resigned himself to his fate, darting a look of rage at Dick, whom he considered the author of his present misfortune.

"This is your book," said the cashier, handing back his rightful property to our hero. "Do you wish to draw out any money?"

"Two dollars," said Dick.

"Very well. Write an order for that amount."

Before doing so, Dick, who now that he saw Travis in the power of the law began to pity him, went up to the officer, and said,—

"Won't you let him go? I've got my bank-book back, and I don't want anything done to him."

"Sorry I can't oblige you," said the officer; "but I'm not allowed to do it. He'll have to stand his trial."

"I'm sorry for you, Travis," said Dick. "I didn't want you arrested. I only wanted my bank-book back."

"Curse you!" said Travis, scowling vindictively. "Wait till I get free. See if I don't fix you."

"You needn't pity him too much," said the officer. "I know him now. He's been on the Island before."

"It's a lie," said Travis, violently.

"Don't be too noisy, my friend," said the officer. "If you've got no more business here, we'll be going."

He withdrew with the prisoner in charge, and Dick, having drawn his two dollars, left the bank. Notwithstanding the violent words the prisoner had used towards himself, and his attempted robbery, he could not help feeling sorry that he had been instrumental in causing his arrest.

"I'll keep my book a little safer hereafter," thought Dick. "Now I must go and see Tom Wilkins."

Before dismissing the subject of Travis and his theft, it may be remarked that he was duly tried, and, his guilt being clear, was sent to Blackwell's Island for nine months. At the end of that time, on his release, he got a chance to work his passage on a ship to San Francisco, where he probably arrived in due time. At any rate, nothing more has been heard of him, and probably his threat of vengeance against Dick will never be carried into effect.

Returning to the City Hall Park, Dick soon fell in with Tom Wilkins.

"How are you, Tom?" he said. "How's your mother?"

"She's better, Dick, thank you. She felt worried about bein' turned out into the street; but I gave her that money from you, and now she feels a good deal easier."

"I've got some more for you, Tom," said Dick, producing a two-dollar bill from his pocket.

"I ought not to take it from you, Dick."

"Oh, it's all right, Tom. Don't be afraid."

"But you may need it yourself."

"There's plenty more where that came from."

"Any way, one dollar will be enough. With that we can pay the rent."

"You'll want the other to buy something to eat."

"You're very kind, Dick."

"I'd ought to be. I've only got myself to take care of."

"Well, I'll take it for my mother's sake. When you want anything done just call on Tom Wilkins."

"All right. Next week, if your mother doesn't get better, I'll give you some more."

Tom thanked our hero very gratefully, and Dick walked away, feeling the self-approval which always accompanies a generous and disinterested action. He was generous by nature, and, before the period at which he is introduced to the reader's notice, he frequently treated his friends to cigars and oyster-stews. Sometimes he invited them to accompany him to the theatre at his expense. But he never derived from these acts of liberality the same degree of satisfaction as from this timely gift to Tom Wilkins. He felt that his money was well bestowed, and would save an entire family from privation and discomfort. Five dollars would, to be sure, make something of a difference in the amount of his savings. It was more than he was able to save up in a week. But Dick felt fully repaid for what he had done, and he felt prepared to give as much more, if Tom's mother should continue to be sick, and should appear to him to need it.

Besides all this, Dick felt a justifiable pride in his financial ability to afford so handsome a gift. A year before, however much he might have desired to give, it would have been quite out of his power to give five dollars. His cash balance never reached that amount. It was seldom, indeed, that it equalled one dollar. In more ways than one Dick was beginning to reap the advantage of his self-denial and judicious economy.

It will be remembered that when Mr. Whitney at parting

with Dick presented him with five dollars, he told him that he might repay it to some other boy who was struggling upward. Dick thought of this, and it occurred to him that after all he was only paying up an old debt.

When Fosdick came home in the evening, Dick announced his success in recovering his lost money, and described the manner in which it had been brought about.

"You're in luck, Dick," said Fosdick. "I guess we'd better not trust the bureau-drawer again."

"I mean to carry my book round with me," said Dick.

"So shall I, as long as we stay at Mrs. Mooney's. I wish we were in a better place."

"I must go down and tell her she needn't expect Travis back. Poor chap, I pity him!"

Travis was never more seen in Mrs. Mooney's establishment. He was owing that lady for a fortnight's rent of his room, which prevented her feeling much compassion for him. The room was soon after let to a more creditable tenant, who proved a less troublesome neighbor than his predecessor.

CHAPTER XXIV

Dick Receives a Letter

It was about a week after Dick's recovery of his bank-book, that Fosdick brought home with him in the evening a copy of the "Daily Sun."

"Would you like to see your name in print, Dick?" he asked.

"Yes," said Dick, who was busy at the wash-stand, endeavoring to efface the marks which his day's work had left upon his hands. "They haven't put me up for mayor, have they? 'Cause if they have, I shan't accept. It would interfere too much with my private business."

"No," said Fosdick, "they haven't put you up for office yet, though that may happen sometime. But if you want to see your name in print, here it is."

Dick was rather incredulous, but, having dried his hands on the towel, took the paper, and following the directions of Fosdick's finger, observed in the list of advertised letters the name of "RAGGED DICK."

"By gracious, so it is," said he. "Do you s'pose it means me?"

"I don't know of any other Ragged Dick,—do you?"

"No," said Dick, reflectively; "it must be me. But I don't know of anybody that would be likely to write to me."

"Perhaps it is Frank Whitney," suggested Fosdick, after a little reflection. "Didn't he promise to write to you?"

"Yes," said Dick, "and he wanted me to write to him."

"Where is he now?"

"He was going to a boarding-school in Connecticut, he said. The name of the town was Barnton."

"Very likely the letter is from him."

"I hope it is. Frank was a tip-top boy, and he was the first that made me ashamed of bein' so ignorant and dirty."

"You had better go to the post-office to-morrow morning, and ask for the letter."

"P'r'aps they won't give it to me."

"Suppose you wear the old clothes you used to a year ago, when Frank first saw you? They won't have any doubt of your being Ragged Dick then."

"I guess I will. I'll be sort of ashamed to be seen in 'em though," said Dick, who had considerable more pride in a neat personal appearance than when we were first introduced to him.

"It will be only for one day, or one morning," said Fosdick.

"I'd do more'n that for the sake of gettin' a letter from Frank. I'd like to see him."

The next morning, in accordance with the suggestion of Fosdick, Dick arrayed himself in the long disused Washington coat and Napoleon pants, which he had carefully preserved, for what reason he could hardly explain.

When fairly equipped, Dick surveyed himself in the mirror,—if the little seven-by-nine-inch looking-glass, with which the room was furnished, deserved the name. The result of the survey was not on the whole a pleasing one. To tell the truth, Dick was quite ashamed of his appearance, and, on opening the chamber-door, looked around to see that the coast was clear, not being willing to have any of his fellow-boarders see him in his present attire.

He managed to slip out into the street unobserved, and, after attending to two or three regular customers who came down-town early in the morning, he made his way down Nassau Street to the post-office. He passed along until he came to a compartment on which he read ADVERTISED LETTERS, and, stepping up to the little window, said,—

"There's a letter for me. I saw it advertised in the 'Sun' yesterday."

"What name?" demanded the clerk.

"Ragged Dick," answered our hero.

"That's a queer name," said the clerk, surveying him a little curiously. "Are you Ragged Dick?"

"If you don't believe me, look at my clo'es," said Dick.

"That's pretty good proof, certainly," said the clerk, laughing. "If that isn't your name, it deserves to be."

"I believe in dressin' up to your name," said Dick.

"Do you know any one in Barnton, Connecticut?" asked the clerk, who had by this time found the letter.

"Yes," said Dick. "I know a chap that's at boardin'-school there."

"It appears to be in a boy's hand. I think it must be yours."

The letter was handed to Dick through the window. He received it eagerly, and drawing back so as not to be in the way of the throng who were constantly applying for letters, or slipping them into the boxes provided for them, hastily opened it, and began to read. As the reader may be interested in the contents of the letter as well as Dick, we transcribe it below.

It was dated Barnton, Conn., and commenced thus—

"Dear Dick—You must excuse my addressing this letter to 'Ragged Dick'; but the fact is, I don't know what your last name is, nor where you live. I am afraid there is not much chance of your getting this letter; but I hope you will. I have thought of you very often, and wondered how you were getting along, and I should have written to you before if I had known where to direct.

"Let me tell you a little about myself. Barnton is a very pretty country town, only about six miles from Hartford. The boarding-school which I attend is under the charge of Ezekiel Munroe, A.M. He is a man of about fifty, a graduate of Yale College, and has always been a teacher. It is a large two-story house, with an addition containing a good many small bed-chambers for the boys. There are about twenty of us, and there is one assistant teacher who teaches the English branches. Mr. Munroe, or Old Zeke, as we call him behind his back, teaches Latin and Greek. I am studying both these languages, because Father wants me to go to college.

"But you won't be interested in hearing about our studies. I will tell you how we amuse ourselves. There are about fifty acres of land belonging to Mr. Munroe; so that we have plenty of room for play. About a quarter of a mile from the house there is a good-sized pond. There is a large, round-bottomed boat, which is stout and strong. Every Wednesday and Saturday afternoon, when the weather is good, we go out rowing on the pond. Mr. Barton, the assistant teacher, goes with us, to look after us. In the summer we are allowed to go in bathing. In the winter there is splendid skating on the pond.

"Besides this, we play ball a good deal, and we have various other plays. So we have a pretty good time, although we study pretty hard too. I am getting on very well in my studies. Father has not decided yet where he will send me to college.

"I wish you were here, Dick. I should enjoy your company, and besides I should like to feel that you were getting an education. I think you are naturally a pretty smart boy; but I suppose, as you have to earn your own living, you don't get much chance to learn. I only wish I had a few hundred dollars of my own. I would have you come up here, and attend school with us. If I ever have a chance to help you in any way, you may be sure that I will.

"I shall have to wind up my letter now, as I have to hand in a composition to-morrow, on the life and character of Washington. I might say that I have a friend who wears a coat that once belonged to the general. But I suppose that coat must be worn out by this time. I don't much like writing compositions. I would a good deal rather write letters.

"I have written a longer letter than I meant to. I hope you will get it, though I am afraid not. If you do, you must be sure to answer it, as soon as possible. You needn't mind if your writing does look like 'hens-tracks,' as you told me once.

"Good-by, Dick. You must always think of me, as your very true friend,

"Frank Whitney"

Dick read this letter with much satisfaction. It is always pleasant to be remembered, and Dick had so few friends that it was more to him than to boys who are better provided. Again, he felt a new sense of importance in having a letter addressed to him. It was the first letter he had ever received. If it had been sent to him a year before, he would not have been able to read it. But now, thanks to Fosdick's instructions, he could not only read writing, but he could write a very good hand himself.

There was one passage in the letter which pleased Dick.

It was where Frank said that if he had the money he would pay for his education himself.

"He's a tip-top feller," said Dick. "I wish I could see him ag'in."

There were two reasons why Dick would like to have seen Frank. One was the natural pleasure he would have in meeting a friend; but he felt also that he would like to have Frank witness the improvement he had made in his studies and mode of life.

"He'd find me a little more 'spectable than when he first saw me," thought Dick.

Dick had by this time got up to Printing House Square. Standing on Spruce Street, near the "Tribune" office, was his old enemy, Micky Maguire.

It has already been said that Micky felt a natural enmity towards those in his own condition in life who wore better clothes than himself. For the last nine months, Dick's neat appearance had excited the ire of the young Philistine. To appear in neat attire and with a clean face Micky felt was a piece of presumption, and an assumption of superiority on the part of our hero, and he termed it "tryin' to be a swell."

Now his astonished eyes rested on Dick in his ancient attire, which was very similar to his own. It was a moment of triumph to him. He felt that "pride had had a fall," and he could not forbear reminding Dick of it.

"Them's nice clo'es you've got on," said he, sarcastically, as Dick came up.

"Yes," said Dick, promptly. "I've been employin' your tailor. If my face was only dirty we'd be taken for twin brothers."

"So you've give up tryin' to be a swell?"

"Only for this partic'lar occasion," said Dick. "I wanted to make a fashionable call, so I put on my regimentals."

"I don't b'lieve you've got any better clo'es," said Micky.

"All right," said Dick, "I won't charge you nothin' for what you believe."

Here a customer presented himself for Micky, and Dick went back to his room to change his clothes, before resuming business.

CHAPTER XXV

Dick Writes His First Letter

W<small>HEN</small> Fosdick reached home in the evening, Dick displayed his letter with some pride.

"It's a nice letter," said Fosdick, after reading it. "I should like to know Frank."

"I'll bet you would," said Dick. "He's a trump."

"When are you going to answer it?"

"I don't know," said Dick dubiously. "I never writ a letter."

"There's no reason why you shouldn't. There's always a first time, you know."

"I don't know what to say," said Dick.

"Get some paper and sit down to it, and you'll find enough to say. You can do that this evening instead of studying."

"If you'll look it over afterwards, and shine it up a little."

"Yes, if it needs it; but I rather think Frank would like it best just as you wrote it."

Dick decided to adopt Fosdick's suggestion. He had very serious doubts as to his ability to write a letter. Like a good many other boys, he looked upon it as a very serious job, not reflecting that, after all, letter-writing is nothing but talking upon paper. Still, in spite of his misgivings, he felt that the letter ought to be answered, and he wished Frank to hear from him. After various preparations, he at last got settled down to his task, and, before the evening was over, a letter was written. As the first letter which Dick had ever produced, and because it was characteristic of him, my readers may like to read it.

Here it is—

"Dear Frank—I got your letter this mornin', and was very glad to hear you hadn't forgotten Ragged Dick. I ain't so ragged as I was. Open-work coats and trousers has gone out of fashion. I put on the Washington coat and Napoleon pants to go to the post-office, for fear they wouldn't think I was the boy that was meant. On my way back I received the congratulations of my intimate friend, Micky Maguire, on my improved appearance.

"I've give up sleepin' in boxes, and old wagons, findin' it didn't agree with my constitution. I've hired a room in Mott Street, and have got a private tooter, who rooms with me and looks after my studies in the evenin'. Mott Street ain't very fashionable; but my manshun on Fifth Avenoo isn't finished yet, and I'm afraid it won't be till I'm a gray-haired veteran. I've got a hundred dollars towards it, which I've saved from my earnin's. I haven't forgot what you and your uncle said to me, and I'm trying to grow up 'spectable. I haven't been to Tony Pastor's, or the Old Bowery, for ever so long. I'd rather save up my money to support me in my old age. When my hair gets gray, I'm goin' to knock off blackin' boots, and go into some light, genteel employment, such as keepin' an apple-stand, or disseminatin' pea-nuts among the people.

"I've got so as to read pretty well, so my tooter

says. I've been studyin' geography and grammar also. I've made such astonishin' progress that I can tell a noun from a conjunction as far away as I can see 'em. Tell Mr. Munroe that if he wants an accomplished teacher in his school, he can send for me, and I'll come on by the very next train. Or, if he wants to sell out for a hundred dollars, I'll buy the whole concern, and agree to teach the scholars all I know myself in less than six months. Is teachin' as good business, generally speakin', as blackin' boots? My private tooter combines both, and is makin' a fortun' with great rapidity. He'll be as rich as Astor some time, *if he only lives long enough.*

"I should think you'd have a bully time at your school. I should like to go out in the boat, or play ball with you. When are you comin' to the city? I wish you'd write and let me know when you do, and I'll call and see you. I'll leave my business in the hands of my numerous clerks, and go round with you. There's lots of things you didn't see when you was here before. They're getting on fast at the Central Park. It looks better than it did a year ago.

"I ain't much used to writin' letters. As this is the first one I ever wrote, I hope you'll excuse the mistakes. I hope you'll write to me again soon. I can't write so good a letter as you; but I'll do my best, as the man said when he was asked if he could swim over to Brooklyn backwards. Good-by, Frank. Thank you for all your kindness. Direct your next letter to No.— Mott Street.

"Your true friend,

"Dick Hunter"

When Dick had written the last word, he leaned back in his chair, and surveyed the letter with much satisfaction.

"I didn't think I could have wrote such a long letter, Fosdick," said he.

"Written would be more grammatical, Dick," suggested his friend.

"I guess there's plenty of mistakes in it," said Dick. "Just look at it, and see."

Fosdick took the letter, and read it over carefully.

"Yes, there are some mistakes," he said; "but it sounds so much like you that I think it would be better to let it go just as it is. It will be more likely to remind Frank of what you were when he first saw you."

"Is it good enough to send?" asked Dick, anxiously.

"Yes, it seems to me to be quite a good letter. It is written just as you talk. Nobody but you could have written such a letter, Dick. I think Frank will be amused at your proposal to come up there as teacher."

"P'r'aps it would be a good idea for us to open a seleck school here in Mott Street," said Dick, humorously. "We could call it 'Professor Fosdick and Hunter's Mott Street Seminary.' Boot-blackin' taught by Professor Hunter."

The evening was so far advanced that Dick decided to postpone copying his letter till the next evening. By this time he had come to have a very fair handwriting, so that when the letter was complete it really looked quite creditable, and no one would have suspected that it was Dick's first attempt in this line. Our hero surveyed it with no little complacency. In fact, he felt rather proud of it, since it reminded him of the great progress he had made. He carried it down to the post-office, and deposited it with his own hands in the proper box. Just on the steps of the building, as he was coming out, he met Johnny Nolan, who had been sent on an errand to Wall Street by some gentleman, and was just returning.

"What are you doin' down here, Dick?" asked Johnny.

"I've been mailin' a letter."

"Who sent you?"

"Nobody."

"I mean, who writ the letter?"

"I wrote it myself."

"Can you write letters?" asked Johnny, in amazement.

"Why shouldn't I?"

"I didn't know you could write. I can't."

"Then you ought to learn."

"I went to school once; but it was too hard work, so I give it up."

"You're lazy, Johnny,—that's what's the matter. How'd you ever expect to know anything, if you don't try?"

"I can't learn."

"You can, if you want to."

Johnny Nolan was evidently of a different opinion. He was a good-natured boy, large of his age, with nothing particularly bad about him, but utterly lacking in that energy, ambition, and natural sharpness for which Dick was distinguished. He was not adapted to succeed in the life which circumstances had forced upon him; for in the street-life of the metropolis a boy needs to be on the alert, and have all his wits about him, or he will find himself wholly distanced by his more enterprising competitors for popular favor. To succeed in his profession, humble as it is, a boot-black must depend upon the same qualities which gain success in higher walks in life. It was easy to see that Johnny, unless very much favored by circumstances, would never rise much above his present level. For Dick, we cannot help hoping much better things.

CHAPTER XXVI

An Exciting Adventure

DICK now began to look about for a position in a store or counting-room. Until he should obtain one he determined to devote half the day to blacking boots, not being willing to break in upon his small capital. He found that he could earn enough in half a day to pay all his necessary expenses, including the entire rent of the room. Fosdick desired to pay his half; but Dick steadily refused, insisting upon paying so much as compensation for his friend's services as instructor.

It should be added that Dick's peculiar way of speaking and use of slang terms had been somewhat modified by his education and his intimacy with Henry Fosdick. Still he continued to indulge in them to some extent, especially when he felt like joking, and it was natural to Dick to joke, as my readers have probably found out by this time. Still his manners were considerably improved, so that he was more likely to obtain a situation than when first introduced to our notice.

Just now, however, business was very dull, and merchants, instead of hiring new assistants, were disposed to part with those already in their employ. After making several ineffectual applications, Dick began to think he should be obliged to stick to his profession until the next season. But about this time something occurred which considerably improved his chances of preferment.

This is the way it happened.

As Dick, with a balance of more than a hundred dollars in the savings bank, might fairly consider himself a young man of property, he thought himself justified in occasionally taking a half holiday from business, and going on an excursion. On Wednesday afternoon Henry Fosdick was sent by his employer on an errand to that part of Brooklyn near Greenwood Cemetery. Dick hastily dressed himself in his best, and determined to accompany him.

The two boys walked down to the South Ferry, and, paying their two cents each, entered the ferry-boat. They remained at the stern, and stood by the railing, watching the great city, with its crowded wharves, receding from view. Beside them was a gentleman with two children—a girl of eight and a little boy of six. The children were talking gayly to their father. While he was pointing out some object of interest to the little girl, the boy managed to creep, unobserved, beneath the chain that extends across the boat, for the protection of passengers, and, stepping incautiously to the edge of the boat, fell over into the foaming water.

At the child's scream, the father looked up, and, with a cry of horror, sprang to the edge of the boat. He would have plunged in, but, being unable to swim, would only have endangered his own life, without being able to save his child.

"My child!" he exclaimed in anguish,—"who will save my child? A thousand—ten thousand dollars to any one who will save him!"

There chanced to be but few passengers on board at the time, and nearly all those were either in the cabins or standing forward. Among the few who saw the child fall was our hero.

Now Dick was an expert swimmer. It was an accomplishment which he had possessed for years, and he no sooner saw the boy fall than he resolved to rescue him. His determination was formed before he heard the liberal offer made by the boy's father. Indeed, I must do Dick the justice to say that, in the excitement of the moment, he did not hear it at all, nor would it have stimulated the alacrity with which he sprang to the rescue of the little boy.

Little Johnny had already risen once, and gone under for the second time, when our hero plunged in. He was obliged to strike out for the boy, and this took time. He reached him none too soon. Just as he was sinking for the third and last time, he caught him by the jacket. Dick was stout and strong, but Johnny clung to him so tightly, that it was with great difficulty he was able to sustain himself.

"Put your arms round my neck," said Dick.

The little boy mechanically obeyed, and clung with a grasp strengthened by his terror. In this position Dick could bear his weight better. But the ferry-boat was receding fast. It was quite impossible to reach it. The father, his face pale with terror and anguish, and his hands clasped in suspense, saw the brave boy's struggles, and prayed with agonizing fervor that he might be successful. But it is probable, for they were now midway of the river, that both Dick and the little boy whom he had bravely undertaken to rescue would have been drowned, had not a row-boat been fortunately near. The two men who were in it witnessed the accident, and hastened to the rescue of our hero.

"Keep up a little longer," they shouted, bending to their oars, "and we will save you."

Dick heard the shout, and it put fresh strength into him. He battled manfully with the treacherous sea, his eyes fixed longingly upon the approaching boat.

"Hold on tight, little boy," he said. "There's a boat coming."

The little boy did not see the boat. His eyes were closed to shut out the fearful water, but he clung the closer to his young preserver. Six long, steady strokes, and the boat dashed along side. Strong hands seized Dick and his youthful burden, and drew them into the boat, both dripping with water.

"God be thanked!" exclaimed the father, as from the steamer he saw the child's rescue. "That brave boy shall be rewarded, if I sacrifice my whole fortune to compass it."

"You've had a pretty narrow escape, young chap," said one of the boatmen to Dick. "It was a pretty tough job you undertook."

"Yes," said Dick. "That's what I thought when I was in the water. If it hadn't been for you, I don't know what would have 'come of us."

"Anyhow you're a plucky boy, or you wouldn't have dared to jump into the water after this little chap. It was a risky thing to do."

"I'm used to the water," said Dick, modestly. "I didn't stop to think of the danger, but I wasn't going to let that little fellow drown without tryin' to save him."

The boat at once headed for the ferry wharf on the Brooklyn side. The captain of the ferry-boat, seeing the rescue, did not think it necessary to stop his boat, but kept on his way. The whole occurrence took place in less time than I have occupied in telling it.

The father was waiting on the wharf to receive his little boy, with what feelings of gratitude and joy can be easily understood. With a burst of happy tears he clasped him to his arms. Dick was about to withdraw modestly, but the gentleman perceived the movement, and, putting down the child, came forward, and, clasping his hand, said with emotion, "My brave boy, I owe you a debt I can never repay. But for your timely service I should now be plunged into an anguish which I cannot think of without a shudder."

Our hero was ready enough to speak on most occasions, but always felt awkward when he was praised.

"It wasn't any trouble," he said, modestly. "I can swim like a top."

"But not many boys would have risked their lives for a stranger," said the gentleman. "But," he added with a sudden thought, as his glance rested on Dick's dripping garments, "both you and my little boy will take cold in wet clothes. Fortunately I have a friend living close at hand, at whose house you will have an opportunity of taking off your clothes, and having them dried."

Dick protested that he never took cold; but Fosdick, who had now joined them, and who, it is needless to say, had been greatly alarmed at Dick's danger, joined in urging compliance with the gentleman's proposal, and in the end our hero had to yield. His new friend secured a hack, the driver of which agreed for extra recompense to receive the dripping boys into his carriage, and they were whirled rapidly to a pleasant house in a side street, where matters were quickly explained, and both boys were put to bed.

"I ain't used to goin' to bed quite so early," thought Dick. "This is the queerest excursion I ever took."

Like most active boys Dick did not enjoy the prospect of spending half a day in bed; but his confinement did not last as long as he anticipated.

In about an hour the door of his chamber was opened, and a servant appeared, bringing a new and handsome suit of clothes throughout.

"You are to put on these," said the servant to Dick; "but you needn't get up till you feel like it."

"Whose clothes are they?" asked Dick.

"They are yours."

"Mine! Where did they come from?"

"Mr. Rockwell sent out and bought them for you. They are the same size as your wet ones."

"Is he here now?"

"No. He bought another suit for the little boy, and has gone back to New York. Here's a note he asked me to give you."

Dick opened the paper, and read as follows—

"Please accept this outfit of clothes as the first instalment of a debt which I can never repay. I have asked to have your wet suit dried, when you can reclaim it. Will you oblige me by calling to-morrow at my counting-room, No.—, Pearl Street.

"Your friend,
"James Rockwell"

CHAPTER XXVII

Conclusion

WHEN Dick was dressed in his new suit, he surveyed his figure with pardonable complacency. It was the best he had ever worn, and fitted him as well as if it had been made expressly for him.

"He's done the handsome thing," said Dick to himself; "but there wasn't no 'casin for his givin' me these clothes. My lucky stars are shinin' pretty bright now. Jumpin' into the water pays better than shinin' boots; but I don't think I'd like to try it more'n once a week."

About eleven o'clock the next morning Dick repaired to Mr. Rockwell's counting-room on Pearl Street. He found himself in front of a large and handsome warehouse. The counting-room was on the lower floor. Our hero entered, and found Mr. Rockwell sitting at a desk. No sooner did that gentleman see him than he arose, and, advancing, shook Dick by the hand in the most friendly manner.

"My young friend," he said, "you have done me so great service that I wish to be of some service to you in return. Tell me about yourself, and what plans or wishes you have formed for the future."

Dick frankly related his past history, and told Mr. Rockwell of his desire to get into a store or counting-room, and of the failure of all his applications thus far. The merchant listened attentively to Dick's statement, and, when he had finished, placed a sheet of paper before him, and, handing him a pen, said, "Will you write your name on this piece of paper?"

Dick wrote in a free, bold hand, the name Richard Hunter. He had very much improved in his penmanship, as has already been mentioned, and now had no cause to be ashamed of it.

Mr. Rockwell surveyed it approvingly.

"How would you like to enter my counting-room as clerk, Richard?" he asked.

Dick was about to say "Bully," when he recollected himself, and answered, "Very much."

"I suppose you know something of arithmetic, do you not?"

"Yes, sir."

"Then you may consider yourself engaged at a salary of ten dollars a week. You may come next Monday morning."

"Ten dollars!" repeated Dick, thinking he must have misunderstood.

"Yes; will that be sufficient?"

"It's more than I can earn," said Dick, honestly.

"Perhaps it is at first," said Mr. Rockwell, smiling; "but I am willing to pay you that. I will besides advance you as fast as your progress will justify it."

Dick was so elated than he hardly restrained himself from some demonstration which would have astonished the merchant; but he exercised self-control, and only said, "I'll try to serve you so faithfully, sir, that you won't repent having taken me into your service."

"And I think you will succeed," said Mr. Rockwell, encouragingly. "I will not detain you any longer, for I have some important business to attend to. I shall expect to see you on Monday morning."

Dick left the counting-room, hardly knowing whether he stood on his head or his heels, so overjoyed was he at the sudden change in his fortunes. Ten dollars a week was to him a fortune, and three times as much as he had expected to obtain at first. Indeed he would have been glad, only the day before, to get a place at three dollars a week. He reflected that with the stock of clothes which he had now on hand, he could save up at least half of it, and even then live better than he had been accustomed to do; so that his little fund in the savings bank, instead of being diminished, would be steadily increasing. Then he was to be advanced if he deserved it. It was indeed a bright prospect for a boy who, only a year before, could neither read nor write, and depended for a night's lodging upon the chance hospitality of an alley-way or old wagon. Dick's great ambition to "grow up 'spectable" seemed likely to be accomplished after all.

"I wish Fosdick was as well off as I am," he thought generously. But he determined to help his less fortunate friend, and assist him up the ladder as he advanced himself.

When Dick entered his room on Mott Street, he discovered that some one else had been there before him, and two articles of wearing apparel had disappeared.

"By gracious!" he exclaimed; "somebody's stole my Washington coat and Napoleon pants. Maybe it's an agent of Barnum's, who expects to make a fortun' by exhibitin' the valooable wardrobe of a gentleman of fashion."

Dick did not shed many tears over his loss, as, in his present circumstances, he never expected to have any further use for the well-worn garments. It may be stated that he afterwards saw them adorning the figure of Micky Maguire; but whether that estimable young man stole them himself, he never ascertained. As to the loss, Dick was rather pleased that it had occurred. It seemed to cut him off from the old vagabond life which he hoped never to resume. Henceforward he meant to press onward, and rise as high as possible.

Although it was yet only noon, Dick did not go out again with his brush. He felt that it was time to retire from business. He would leave his share of the public patronage to other boys less fortunate than himself. That evening Dick and Fosdick had a long conversation. Fosdick rejoiced heartily in his friend's success, and on his side had the pleasant news to communicate that his pay had been advanced to six dollars a week.

"I think we can afford to leave Mott Street now," he continued. "This house isn't as neat as it might be, and I should like to live in a nicer quarter of the city."

"All right," said Dick. "We'll hunt up a new room tomorrow. I shall have plenty of time, having retired from business. I'll try to get my reg'lar customers to take Johnny Nolan in my place. That boy hasn't any enterprise. He needs somebody to look out for him."

"You might give him your box and brush, too, Dick."

"No," said Dick; "I'll give him some new ones, but mine I want to keep, to remind me of the hard times I've had, when I was an ignorant boot-black, and never expected to be anything better."

"When, in short, you were 'Ragged Dick.' You must drop that name, and think of yourself now as—"

"Richard Hunter. Esq.," said our hero, smiling.

"A young gentleman on the way to fame and fortune," added Fosdick.

Here ends the story of Ragged Dick. As Fosdick said, he is Ragged Dick no longer. He has taken a step upward, and is determined to mount still higher. There are fresh adventures in store for him, and for others who have been introduced in these pages. Those who have felt interested in his early life

will find his history continued in a new volume, forming the
second of the series, to be called—

FAME AND FORTUNE

or,

THE PROGRESS OF RICHARD HUNTER.

Afterword

In the second half of the nineteenth century, New York City experienced a population explosion. From 1850 to 1870, the city doubled in numbers, from just over five hundred thousand to almost one million, the result of an enormous influx of immigrants from Ireland, Germany, and elsewhere. Tenement districts in what are now Chinatown and the Lower East Side filled to bursting. Working-class entertainments—not just the Bowery Theater, originally touted by the city's mayor in the 1820s as a form of social uplift for working-class audiences, but also bowling saloons, oyster houses, dance halls, gambling dens, and brothels—rose to meet new demands. Streets became contested public spaces as tenement dwellers spent more time in them. Child homelessness became a threat both real and imagined, with numbers probably inflated to account for children who middle-class reformers assumed should be at home but rarely were, for understandable reasons. In 1845, the city established its first professional police force; in 1852, a group of Methodist reformers tore down the infamous Old Brewery in the district known as the Five Points—by then one of the world's most notorious slums—and replaced it with a mission. The Five Points House of Industry, established nearby, attempted to

educate and otherwise serve the needs of New York's prolif-
erating homeless youth, many of whom scrambled to make
their livings as rag pickers, match boys, bootblacks, or pros-
titutes. The same population was served by the Newsboys'
Lodging House, which Charles Loring Brace opened in
1854 above of the offices of the *New York Sun* on Fulton
Street.

The literature produced in response to the problem of
homelessness and urban poverty—we might call it, borrowing the subtitle of Alger's novel, the literature of "Street Life
in New York"—varies widely, ranging from sensational
sketches to reformist tracts to philosophical meditations.
The working-class hero Mose, the strapping Bowery B'hoy
fireman, first appeared on stage in Benjamin Baker's 1848
play, *A Glance at New York*, but soon became an urban folk
hero and a patron saint to Bowery tramps. That same year,
E. Z. C. Judson—aka Ned Buntline—published *The Mysteries and Miseries of New York*, a liberal adaptation of Eu-
gène Sue's serialized novel *Les Mystères de Paris* (1842–43),
helping to draw attention to the darker corners of urban life.
Newspaper writers such as George Foster produced guide-
books to the city's underworld for armchair slummers
(*New-York by Gaslight*, 1850). Herman Melville's classic
story "Bartleby, the Scrivener" (1853) features a young
copyist in a Wall Street law firm who refuses to leave the
office in which he has been employed, effectively becoming
a squatter until he is hauled away to Manhattan's notorious
prison, the Tombs.

Appearing fifteen years later, Horatio Alger's first and most
famous novel takes quite a different approach to street life and
business culture. Alger is most famous, of course, for having
defined the "pull yourself up by your bootstraps," "rags-to-
riches" formula in American fiction, and the novel drips with
advice for young readers about how to get ahead while avoiding the city's temptations and moral pitfalls. In many ways,

Alger offers a scrubbed-up version of the city mysteries literature that preceded it. Serving as a tour guide for the wealthy son of a New York businessman, "Ragged" Dick refuses, unlike George Foster's narrators, to explore the city's darker corners or scenes of vice and depravity. And in contrast to Melville's Bartleby, Dick is gung ho to get ahead, obsequiously pandering to the sentimental side of kindly merchant-class patrons. Melville's Bartleby stands as a critique of corporate business culture—of office space, and the capitalist economy it represents—which deadens the mind, robs the soul, and prevents true sympathy. Bartleby—who, like Dick Hunter, is homeless—rejects notions of private property and prevailing understandings of labor relations. He refuses to agree to the rules of the workplace; he also refuses subjection to life on the streets. And the story's narrator—the lawyer who is Bartleby's erstwhile employer—can't handle it. He has certain assumptions about how property works and Bartleby prefers not to play by those rules. With this contrast in mind, we might think of Dick as a pair with Bartleby—but perhaps as the anti-Bartleby.

A benign version of the city swindler stereotype, Dick in fact proves his virtue by playing by the rules, not by resisting them. Moreover, as Michael Meyer points out in the introduction to this volume, Dick reads his way into upward mobility, setting aside money from his earnings for good books, whose protagonists he can emulate. (We can only assume that *Ragged Dick* itself aspired to be such a volume.) Through the first part of the novel, Alger's dirty-faced but attractive hero overhears his businessmen clients talking and mimics them, opening a window onto how nineteenth-century corporate capitalism worked: Consider his constant references to important connections and friends, or the way in which he, like P. T. Barnum, traffics in association with the memory of General Washington, almost seven decades dead. Significantly, Dick imitates the successful people in his surroundings rather than satirizing them. He keeps a sharp eye out, not simply for his personal safety, but for a chance to get ahead. Unlike Bartleby, Dick is all too willing to take a job as a clerk the first chance he gets.

Dick's street smarts make him a useful tour guide for Frank Whitney and turn the novel itself into a handbook not just for business but also for greenhorns or tourists on how to survive in the city. Especially in its early chapters, the novel functions as a literal guide to city landmarks and landscapes. If you read this book and were growing up in Philadelphia or Hartford or Columbus or Columbia, Missouri, you could easily have used it to learn the names of famous places, their locations and appearances. You would learn handy facts, such as twenty city blocks make a mile. You would also know how to avoid some of the cons for which New York was famous. In "Bartleby, the Scrivener," which was subtitled "A Story of Wall Street," the story's setting seems to be symbolic, with Wall Street a synecdoche for the city's new business culture; in Alger's novel we're very literally told where to go and not to go if we're interested in being upwardly mobile or staying morally pure. Alger's streets—not just the business culture that inhabits their buildings—are contested spaces, sometimes mean, and something from which one needs to be saved.

As a print genre, tour books were called into existence by the city's extraordinary growth. Dozens of books promised to expose readers not just to the streets' dark corners but also to the inner workings of the upper and lower classes. This was the literature of sunshine and shadow. By exposing the lives of the decadent wealthy or the unseemly poor—the upper ten and the lower million—such books promised mastery of the city's new extremes and access to interior spaces that most New Yorkers, let alone readers from outside the city, could only imagine.

Other genres sought to mediate the city for newcomers.

Sermons intended for young men flowing in from the hinter-
lands focused on the seductive dangers of the streets. The
Reverend Henry Ward Beecher's *Lectures to Young Men: On
Various Important Subjects*, a bestseller starting in the 1840s,
warned against the dangers of the city "sharper," a young
man who would ingratiate himself to a newcomer from out of
town, only to lead him to gambling and drink, take his savings, and leave him to shame and possibly suicide. Such mor-
alizing was darker and more sensationalistic than Alger ever
waxed. "The moment the inexperienced youth sets his foot
on the sidewalk of the city," wrote the Reverend John Todd in
1850, "he is marked and watched by eyes that he never
dreamed of. The boy who cries his penny-paper, and the old
woman at her table professedly selling a few apples and a
little gingerbread, are not all who watch him. There is the
seducer in the shape of the young man who came before him,
and who has already lost the last remains of shame."

Such tracts and sermons warned that young people could
not resist the street's seductive pull. This says a lot about the
nature of the streets, but also about reformers' views of human nature—especially the nature of young boys. At play
here is a growing evangelical Christian notion of selfhood:
that "self"—human nature—needs to be denied, restrained,
controlled. This evangelical ideology of self-control is bound
tightly with a new middle-class identity, a fear that what boys
would *naturally* do is act like the working class. (Think about
other "boy books" from the period, such as Mark Twain's,
and imagine the trouble his characters would get into in New
York.) But this literature focuses on young men from the
middle class who might fall victim to the vices of the lower.
Alger reverses this emphasis, focusing on the redeeming
qualities of working-class street youth, the bootblacks and
newsboys who might be saved and made productive citizens
rather than left to a life of crime.

As many critics have noted, *Ragged Dick* doesn't investigate the structural causes of poverty or inequality, the reason some young men headed to the city to seek their fortune while others scrambled to survive on the streets. In Alger's world, street and countinghouse are much the same: Success in either arena, or the passage from one to the other, is due to know-how, a desire for personal improvement, and the savvy to take the right chance when it presents itself. But street life—homelessness and the working-class struggle for survival—*was* a real problem in the nineteenth century, on a greater scale than most contemporary Americans can imagine, especially where children were concerned.

In 1849 the city's first chief of police, George Mastell, claimed that ten thousand "idle and vicious children of both sexes . . . infest our public thoroughfares" (qtd. in Stansell). Some put the number as high as forty thousand. This report inspired Charles Loring Brace, later founder of the Newsboys' Lodging House, to establish the Children's Aid Society in 1853. Reformers like Brace felt that working-class and immigrant mothers did not live up to their ideals of domesticity and motherhood. As the historian Christine Stansell has demonstrated, middle-class evangelical reformers were blind to the family-based economy of working-class life, which required kids to contribute to household income by scavenging or working as newsies, bootblacks, or match sellers. The Children's Aid Society removed 250,000 children from the city between 1853 and 1929—even children who had homes and families—and shipped them by train to the Midwest or West, where they would be adopted by good Protestant families. (Johnny Nolan in this novel seems narrowly to have escaped such a fate.)

Street children were at the heart of what Brace called "the dangerous classes of New York," which was also the title of his major literary effort, published in 1872. Brace told his readers that street urchins were like rats: "too quick and cunning to be often caught in their petty plunderings, so they gnawed away at the foundations of society undisturbed." But when he wrote about individual street boys, rather than the collective problem, or when he addressed them directly, he often used cheerier terms that sound more like Alger's descriptions of dirty but magnetic youngsters. In language that seems to be directly influenced by *Ragged Dick*, Brace writes: "With a boy, 'Arab of the streets,' one always has the consolation that, despite his ragged clothes and bed in a box or hay-barge, he often has a rather good time of it, and enjoys many of the delicious pleasures of a child's roving life, and that a fortunate turn of events may at any time make an honest, industrious fellow of him." Brace demonstrates here that his notions of masculinity—what we might think of as a distinction between Broadway and Bowery, middle-class and working-class manhood—shape his understanding of street life. What good American boy, after all, wouldn't want to *be* Ragged Dick, free from adult supervision, never having to bathe or cut his hair, probably growing up to be a manly swell like Mose. This is one reason Alger's fiction—and other "boy books," including Mark Twain's novels—was controversial in its own day. Genteel library boards, as the literary historian Glenn Hendler has shown, felt that Alger's fiction did more harm than good, that boys would be *attracted* to Dick's freedom rather than his rise to respectability. Books like Alger's were so controversial, in fact, that the Library Association of America held special meetings on the topic of children's literature in 1879.

If such worries seem unfounded, it's because Alger's heroes aspire to respectability and domesticity as much as they do to success in business. It seems no coincidence that Dick, in his capacity as tour guide, spends more time on sunshine than shadow. When he is enlisted to show Frank Whitney the city, he sticks to civic monuments and places of respectable entertainment, even if his knowledge is confined chiefly to exteriors rather than interiors of such establishments and in-

stitutions. Instead of showing the dark recesses of the Five
Points or taking him to the Old Bowery, he shows Frank the
city's great public and commercial buildings: the Astor Hotel, city hall, Barnum's Museum, etc., all the way uptown.
That is, he shows Frank public spaces—monuments to civic
virtue—rather than hotbeds of private vice. It's no accident,
then, that their trek uptown has as its final destination the
new Central Park.

For moral reformers, one antidote to street life lay in creat-
ing a different kind of public space, one where classes would
ideally intermingle—to the uplifting benefit of the poor in
particular. The quintessential example of this new kind of
public space would be Central Park, designed by Brace's good
friend Frederick Law Olmstead. But as Hendler points out,
when Dick and Frank actually get to Central Park it's a bit of
a disappointment. Like Dick, the Park is still rather rough and
undeveloped. It needs improving, is still under construction—
and, in fact, so is Dick; when he writes Frank a letter near the
end of the novel, he's able to report on the progress both he
and the Park are making.

As Hendler argues, the parallel Alger draws between
Dick and the Park is consistent with the Park Commissioners' plans for improving the lower classes. The Park would
be the opposite of the working-class street culture of the
Lower East Side. It would refine its patrons the same way
Frank affects Dick: it would model gentility and in doing so
hold out the promise of upward mobility.

At the heart of debates about street culture and the problem of homeless youth were old and new notions of manhood. In the older version, manliness meant the social status
of the gentleman, founded in self-control. Gentlemen wore
kid gloves and had delicate manners. The new model of
American manhood was more muscular, more mischievous,
more akin to Bowery life than Broadway refinement. Like
Huck Finn, the new American manhood chafed at overcivili-

zation. "Boyhood," for this new style of manliness, became analogous to uncivilized wilderness. This nostalgic appeal of the street boy's freedom shines through Alger's novel. But *Ragged Dick*'s appeal is also a classic act of bait and switch. The novel hooks young readers—perhaps their fathers as well—and then reels them in to an ideal of respectability. In achieving an economically successful young manhood by the novel's end, Dick doesn't just prefer to be more obsequious than Bartleby or willfully submit to the kind of civilizing influence represented by Mark Twain's Widow Douglas. Instead, Dick conflates his manhood with a very specific kind of economic security that values domestic space over wilderness, even as it retains a nostalgic trace of savage boyhood.

It shouldn't come as a shock to hear that *Ragged Dick* is, in the end, about business culture. As the great Americanist critic Alan Trachtenberg wrote in an introduction to an earlier Signet Classics edition of this novel, "The name Horatio Alger has come down to us as *the* synonym for capitalist ideology." Dick is already good at business when the novel starts; he just needs instructions on how to clean up and move up the ladder. But as the critic Michael Moon has shown in what is perhaps the most influential modern reading of the novel, the closer we examine Dick's trajectory, the more we realize that Alger's fiction isn't many of the things it's popularly understood to be. Alger's fictions are often taken to be rags-to-riches stories. But on closer examination, they don't bear out this plot precisely. His characters, for one thing, become *respectable*, not rich. And their transformations are largely externally bestowed: Protagonists gain the favor of a benevolent patron or dive from a ferry boat, as in Dick's case, to save the child of a wealthy merchant and then receive a reward. Alger's heroes *are* industrious; they *are* eager learners; but *then* they get lucky—by being in the right place at the right time; and above all, their defining characteristic is their obsequiousness: These are narratives of luck and pluck more than rags to riches.

Ragged Dick, as Moon argues so persuasively, offers a shrewder insight into corporate capitalist culture than the simplistic rags-to-riches mythology would allow. Dick understands, as already noted, the importance of *connections*: Think of the many times he jokingly presents himself as having particular friends in high places. But more important, he understands the importance of playing off older men's nostalgia for youth and independence, which helps explain the pederastic tone modern readers often find in Alger's novels. For decades scholars have been aware that Alger's move from Massachusetts to New York in 1866 was fueled by a clergy sex-abuse scandal: Alger had allegedly committed "unnatural" acts with boys in his congregation. This revelation has led some critics to be suspicious, then, of his attractions to the Newsboys' Lodging House once he arrived in New York or his choice of the "boy book" as a genre for his fictional output.

But biographical circumstances aside, Alger's creation of street urchin heroes who are, without exception, good-looking beneath their dirty exterior resonates with larger cultural patterns that underwrite business culture. Moon makes a similar point by noting the Algeresque language in one of Brace's *Sermons to News Boys*: "Though you are half men in some ways, you are mere children in others. You hunger as much as other children for affection, but you would never tell of it, and hardly understand it yourselves. You miss a friend, somebody to care for you. It is true you are becoming rapidly toughened to friendlessness; still you would be very, very glad, if you could have one true and warm friend." Compare that passage with the exchange between Dick and Frank just before they reach Central Park or with the novel's opening sequence. There's a pattern of tender expression, accompanied by a physical caress or touch, fraternal or perhaps paternal affection that, as modeled by Mr. Greyson waking Dick in the novel's opening pages, recognizes Dick's potential to rise above the circumstances of the street.

On this reading, *Ragged Dick* reveals the intimate and intergenerational relations between men that define capitalist culture, the desires that reproduce corporate structures. But it also figures these relations as a new, exclusively male domesticity. Consider the title for chapter XX: "Nine Months Later." That is, nine months after Dick and Fosdick move in together, they give birth to a "nest egg" of their own. (In a later volume they even adopt, for a time, a younger child, Mark the Match Boy.) This homosocial, business-class domesticity—the replacement of family ties by business associations described in fraternal or paternal terms—reveals the networks of intimacy, affection, and desires that structure capitalist culture. In Moon's words, "Alger's all-boy families merely imitate the extraordinary propensities for self-reproduction, for apparently asexual breeding, that they are represented as discovering already ongoing in their first accumulations of capital." Dick "always had an eye for business," we're told over and over from the moment we meet him. He knew how to "look sharp" in both senses of the word. He transitions easily from being a saved boy to being a savior—like Brace and his ilk—of boys, spontaneous generators of capitalist citizenship. Recognizing the role played by Dick's good looks and his willingness to charm older men leaves us with a picture of how business culture works that is, perhaps, more accurate than the rags-to-riches ideology with which Alger has been identified for so long.

—Bryan Waterman

References

Beecher, Henry Ward. *Seven Lectures to Young Men, on Various Important Subjects* (Indianapolis: Thomas B. Cutler, 1844).

Bederman, Gail. *Manliness and Civilization: A Cultural History of Gender and Race in the United States, 1880–1917* (Chicago: University of Chicago Press, 1995).

Brace, Charles Loring. *The Dangerous Classes of New York and Twenty Years' Work Among Them* (New York: Wynkoop and Hallenbeck, 1872).

Gilfoyle, Timothy J. "Street-Rats and Gutter-Snipes: Child Pickpockets and Street Culture in New York City, 1850–1900," *Journal of Social History* 37.4 (2004) 853–62.

Hendler, Glenn. "Pandering in the Public Sphere: Masculinity and the Market in Horatio Alger," *American Quarterly* 48.3 (1996): 415–38.

Moon, Michael. "'The Gentle Boy from the Dangerous Classes': Pederasty, Domesticity, and Capitalism in Horatio Alger," *Representations*, No. 19 (Summer, 1987): 87–110.

Stansell, Christine. *City of Women: Sex and Class in New York, 1789–1860* (New York: Knopf, 1986).

Todd, John. *The Young Man: Hints Addressed to the Young Men of the United States* (Northampton, MA: J. H. Butler, 1845).

Selected Bibliography

Gruber, Frank. *Horatio Alger, Jr.: A Biography and Bibliography.* Grover Jones Press: West Los Angeles, 1961.

Hendler, Glenn. "Pandering in the Public Sphere: Masculinity and the Market in Horatio Alger." *American Quarterly* 48 (1966), 415–38.

Moon, Michael. "'The Gentle Boy from the Dangerous Classes': Pederasty, Domesticity, and Capitalism in Horatio Alger." *Representations* 19 (1987), 87–110.

Nackenoff, Carol. *The Fictional Republic: Horatio Alger and American Political Discourse.* New York: Oxford University Press, 1994.

Schornhorst, Gary. *Horatio Alger, Jr.* Boston: Twayne, 1980.

—— with Jack Bayles. *The Lost Life of Horatio Alger, Jr.* Bloomington: Indiana University Press, 1985.